Sean

The Scarlet Bastards

The Cardinal of Gleann Ceallach

Published By:
Sean P. MacÚisdin on Amazon.com

Dedicated to my muse, colleague, and good friend,
Allan Crossley.

Part One
Nana Armstrong

My grandmother, Nana Armstrong, bore a great resemblance to her distant kin from the ancient Scottish Borders. A tough, leathery harridan with a tongue like a bullwhip and a wolverine's disposition, she was a creature of spectacular resilience and survival who could stare down a NASA Stellar Ranger or a parking lot attendant with equal ease. Her ancestors had been inhabitants of Canada for well over five generations, coming off the boat in the late 1940's and spending most of that time in and around British Columbia's Okanagan Valley in particular, and the expansive Thompson Plateau in general. Yet, after 150 years of Canadian acclimatization, Nana continued to doggedly demonstrate the peculiar and sometimes romantic characteristics of that ancient Border clan with a tenacity unknown in our modern, global society.

Nana Armstrong's appearance was that of a regal vulture whose magnificent coal black hair still stood out amidst the growing grey as did her deep brown eyes which were expressive not in grandmotherly joy nor pride, but in perpetual and stoic gravity. Her personality dominated a room like an imperious headmistress with a drill sergeant's demand for exactitude and a demeanour that addressed failure in only the most cutting of terms. Whether this was the result of some surviving genetic trait that had allowed the Armstrongs to endure the distant turbulent and violent history of their native land, or a more modern rebuttal of the carefree worldview so common amongst my generation, Nana Armstrong was a rare force who tyrannized my formative years.

She was a regular visitor in my youth; Nana Armstrong lived alone in a cottage outside of Cawston, a village east of Keremeos in the southern Okanagan Valley. After the death of my grandfather she was quite content to live her nun-like existence in that windblown kiln of a town; a desiccated and decrepit area slowly being consumed by the desert. The birth of her only grandchild, however, was enough to pry her from her fastidious efforts to maintain a small orchard of McIntosh apples and bring her north on occasion to the town of Naramata, on the eastern bench of Okanagan Lake. It was during those early years, when my parents spent most of their waking hours labouring to make a success of their hobby winery, that Nana inflicted herself upon me.

"Alexander Rutherford Armstrong," delivered in a stern guttural growl that sounded like the proverbial voice of God, was the usual beginning of a chastisement designed to curb some childish behaviour that I was exhibiting. "If you wish to splash in that bathtub like an animal, I will take you onto the back lawn and hose you down like a muddy dog." Or, "Alexander Rutherford Armstrong, if it is your desire to eat with your filthy elbows on the table, I will take you onto the back yard and place your food in the dog dish and you may consume it on the lawn." Nana had a secret love of our backyard; verdant green and thick with Kentucky Bluegrass, it was a polar opposite to the arid wasteland surrounding her small orchard. I had a sneaking suspicion that she also bore no ill will to the family dog, a thick-witted collie named Thunder. (I named it for the gas it had had as a puppy) Her threats, therefore, to dragoon me out onto the lawn to languish with the dog were hollow, but when delivered with the gravity of a figure skating judge, they were more than enough to motivate, at least temporarily, an effort to curb my youthful enthusiasms.

As I grew older and Nana spent more time with us, I grew to know the curious nature of her beliefs and morality – a wondrous amalgamation of the modern and the ancient. For one, she was an avowed Anglican, a rarity in the day when religion was viewed as a fading social disease somewhat like syphilis, or good manners, and she had little use for the *ists* that plagued the world. "Alexander Rutherford Armstrong," she would begin, "you will eat those pancakes like a Christian and not slop syrup around the table. Jesus never slopped his syrup, as you would know if you had read the Bible. Only atheists would make such an unholy mess." I'm not sure how she knew that – Jesus not slopping his syrup, I mean – but she stated it with such an indisputable force of will, that I was not in a position to argue. "Honestly, Alexander." Nana never called me Alex as the rest of the world did. "I expect you to walk like a Christian, not shuffle along with your hands in your pockets. And stop picking your nose; Jesus never picked his nose. Only a humanist would shove his finger in his nose. Stop it this instant." There was no arguing the point, of course; the surety of the statement was conclusive and I was convinced that Jesus was not a boy to pick and flick boogers. I've since changed my mind now that I've matured. I suspect Joseph's nagging of Jesus not to fart, pick his nose, or scratch his arse was simply omitted from the Bible for propriety's sake.

Of course, Nana was even more unusual in her devout support of the arcane institution of the British monarchy. A monarchist in the late 2080's was indeed a rare creature, like a supporter of the Senate, or a fan of the Maple Leafs. They were usually the subject of jest as they waved their miniature Union Jacks at some obscure royal life-event. I recall her severe, thin-lipped enthusiasm at the birth of some nameless royal; the images of a squalling tow-headed babe in swaddling displayed on the television had her waving her little flag like a riding crop at the Queen's Plate as she stood proud of the latest generation of what the rest of the world deemed as social parasites. To suggest such in her presence was to summon the wrath of an Old World deity whose power over the elements meant certain destruction of the transgressor.

One afternoon, whilst Nana was sitting in our living room and knitting me a sweater, a friend of my father who was there to watch the Grey Cup lamented the cost of the Royals spending yet another summer vacation on Mars touring the city of Olympus.

"Mr. Edwards," she delivered in a stern monotone dirge that electrified the room, "if you'd rather live under the thumb of the Republican masses as they hoist up some weak-chinned, moist-handed, milquetoast at the behest of a political party dominated by corporate sharks, industrial piranhas, and backroom baboons, you are always free to emigrate south to the United States where history abounds with that sort of thing."

She was no fan of the Cromwellians either, a fringe party in England bound to remove the monarchy and cut the last few social and political ties to royalty. To raise the name of Richard Lebrun, the party's leader, in her presence was to poke an already very angry bear. "A Frenchman," she would seethe, "who would chastise Queen Victoria III and be supported by the English mob, is the very example of what is wrong with this world!" The fact that Lebrun was an eighth generation Englishman lamenting yet another photograph of the Queen smoking Martian marijuana cigars, or dancing in a club to some bizarre industrial techno beat, or piling yet another Buggati into a tree because of one too many glasses of Tokay, was all beside the point and quite irrelevant. Victoria III was the Queen of Western Canada, warts and all, and no foreigner, irrespective of how many generations his family had lived in England, had the right to tell England what to do.

One can see by my few examples how Nana was a very powerful presence in my youth. She demanded subservience while promoting independence of thought. She lectured on manners and mannerisms, defied modern conventions by making me wear a tie and hold doors open for women, and she taught arcane and romantic traditions with dogged fanaticism. That she died alone one afternoon of a stroke in her orchard was haunting for me, and at the time, oddly relevant to my future.

Two years later, all of her formative tools had made me into the young man who decided on a cool damp evening in February, 2098, that I'd had enough, at the age of 17, of the buttoned-down life and my parents' expectations for me to attend college upon graduation from high school in the summer. I decided to hop a train to Coquitlam and enlist in the United Nations Off-World Legion. Two months later I found myself in the colony of Samsāra, in orbit around Delta Pavonis Prime, some 20 light years from Earth.

If Nana could have seen what she'd created, I suspect she would have been proud, in her miserable, God-fearing, anti-Republican way.

Part Two
"Here's to panties, hoss."

My first view of the fishing village of Agarum was hardly a positive one. Built at the mouth of Aebbas Vallis and with a layout like a handful of tossed dice, the village was an eccentric collection of slab-sided buildings, abandoned shipping containers, tents, tarps, yurts, and the ever-curious dry stone hovels topped with rotten inverted boats for rooves. There were a trio of spindly jetties poking out like daggers into the dark, freezing waters of the Seleucus Lacus where rowboats, dories, keelboats, schooners, punts, pirogues, junks, and gundalows packed them in bobbing chromatic ranks. The rock and sand beach, choked already with a thousand years of deadfalls and branches that had washed down the Aebbas Flumen river, was a garbage dump of detritus from the fishing village; rotting nets, nameless bits of wood and machinery, the partially burnt hull of a decrepit paddlewheeler, and a pair of half-sunk and rusting boilers surrounded a rough-hewn fish processing plant the size of a curling rink. The whole place reeked of rotting fish which was of little surprise as the effluent poured out at an astonishing rate into the water amidst the jetties. How I kept my lunch down I'll never know.

The town was built on an ancient river delta – the site of thousands of years of accumulation of sand and rock that had been worn away from the Aebbas Vallis until that moment in time when the river shifted itself a few hundred meters south to leave the mouth of the vallis exposed. The vallis, some 10 kilometres in length and U-shaped from glacial action thousands of years before, lay between two towering ridges. Bare and craggy, Oxus Mons to the south and Solis Mons to the north were powerful brooding sentinels whose height and treacherous sheer cliffs kept unwanted visitors out while protecting the inhabitants of the vallis from the worst of Samsāra's horrific weather. Trees grew thickly in the vallis, tall Pavonis pine, 20 meters in height with a mushroom-shaped canopy of branches, while brush and ferns choked the forest floor. On occasion, a thin beam of milky light might intrude; a solitary visitor that was quickly overwhelmed by the gloom of the ever-present low cloud of the vallis.

The vallis was an Eden of sorts, a sylvan paradise, dark and cool, beneath the canopy that kept the worst of the heavy winter snows from the forest floor. After a few years of human occupation, however, this Eden was beginning to disappear as the forest was replaced in favour of farmland for crops. Where the river was once shrouded by the gloom of the forest, the treeline was now pushed back by several hundred meters towards the rising sides of the vallis, and genetically modified crops of wheat, oats, barley, rye, and others that had been designed to grow quickly in the cool damp summers, were now ready for harvest.

This first impression never altered as I hopped off a barge laden with a couple of dozen head of Scottish highland cattle, the herd of food and milk cattle from the cantonment of Ophir Castrum many kilometres to the south. Myself and five *wallahs*, 10 – 15 year old children who were non-combatants signed up in the United Nations Off-World Legion as dogsbodies and gophers, had endured two days on the small barge amidst the lowing of the miserable cattle (the more spacious barge originally chartered had sunk on the way back from the village of Ister in the north). As I vomited my way north from Ophir (I was prone to seasickness as much as carsickness, airsickness, and even camelsickness) I ruminated on the misadventure that had struck me, for herding a score of highland cattle in the Serberor Campus north to Ophir was but the latest of the curious tasks I had undertaken in the six months since my arrival on Samsāra. That that lengthy list had included such terrifying highlights as storming a Tong fort, ambushing a Black Hand patrol with a company of Gliesiun warriors, and fighting off pirates from a grounded paddlewheeler, was simply beside the point. Cattle herding or trench warfare with Tongs – those were the absurd events that underscored the madness of my brief existence there in the year 2098.

On that cool autumn morning, however, with a penetrating drizzle falling from the low glowering ceiling of iron grey cloud, it was the events with a barge and a herd of   highland cattle being goaded onto the beach that was the adventure coming to a satisfying conclusion. The tugboat captain, some jolly Romanian bargee with a grey beard down to his belly, laughed as I and my five *wallahs* led the animals off of our conveyance. On the beach, a crew of stevedores smiled in amusement as they waited to move the animals into pens on the eastern side of the village. That satisfying end, by the way, was the culmination of a terrifying adventure – a mission, my first mission in command mind, to move the decuria's herd from the valley of Alba Vallis south of the cantonment of Ophir Castrum – our home until a week before – north to the town of Ophir and the waiting barge. It was a laughable military assignment given to me with much glee by the subedar of our decuria, a captain in any other military, by the name of Angus Motshegwa, a Capetown Zulu raised by a Scottish missionary, who was known more affectionately as MacShaka, the Tartan Zulu.

It should have been simple – one of the reasons it was assigned to me I'm sure – the six of us on camelback herding the cows north, but it was complicated by events; everything I did seemed to be complicated by events. On the first night of picking up the herd one of my *wallahs* fell asleep on sentry and a band of

Black Hand bravos, the most powerful of a number of Tong and Triad gangs that operated in the colony, slipped in and stole the herd with a plan to move them south to a tiny mining camp to sell for slaughter. It was a bold plan and it would have been easily accomplished had I and my *wallahs*, with the aid of a stoned California drop-out who'd come to the colony on a college break, not managed to sneak in and steal the herd back. It was a proud moment in my brief career with the Legion, that successful completion of my first mission. That pride evaporated, however, upon our arrival at Agarum – blown away by a chuckling naique, a Legion corporal in faded scarlet *salwar* trousers and cobalt blue *sherwani* coat, sent to pick us up.

"Finally fuckin' got he'e did you?" asked the naique, an evil looking Han Chinese named Ling Bi-jun. He was lounging against a clapboard shack smoking a cigar as the cows were unloaded from the barge. The *wallahs*, led by one of their own, a 15 year old bloodthirsty Jezebel with some romantic aspirations for me, named Jindan Chandrakala, gathered around Ling, saluted and fawned over him, forgetting me as quickly as a wedding vow in Las Vegas. It hurt my feelings, I'll admit. Only days before I had led the little brutes in a midnight raid on a Black Hand camp to liberate our stolen herd, and though Jindan provided most of the real leadership and planning, I was still the face of the plan's implementation and success. To see them then, rallying around the acidic naique sent to meet us and forgetting our shared adventure certainly stung, and it was made worse a moment later when Ling announced, "I on'y have room for *wallahs*. Ca'go to cast'um take up a' the room in the t'uck. You can ride you' came' to cast'um o' wait fo' me to come back."

This was delivered with such smug snottiness – I was a mere *guǐlǎo* and a rather useless one at that – that I instantly bristled with indignity and replied with borderline insubordination, "I'll wait for the ride, thanks." No *Huzūra*, no other honourifics, no toadying of any kind – it was sauce, the type of sauce that could have easily landed me a few blows to the face. The naique didn't bite, however; he merely smiled.

"Be back in few hou' then." He gathered the *wallahs* and walked off, save for Jindan who came over and flashed that charming gap-toothed smile of hers.

"*Sirdar*," it was her nickname for me, meaning "general" or some such thing, "do not be angry. The *wallahs* are tired and excited to see the new castrum. Do you wish me to stay with you?" This was said as she held and patted my hand, like my mother might have done had she'd seen me picked last for softball.

"No," I replied, mollified somewhat. "You go with them and make sure they don't drive the naique crazy. I'll wait in town here."

"Are you sure, *Sirdar*?" she asked prettily. She smiled again, perhaps a bit coy now. Her doe eyes seemed larger and she squeezed my hand. Goodness, I thought with rising panic, nothing good will come of this.

"No, go ahead. I'll see you at supper."

Jindan seemed disappointed though she still smiled. She turned to depart, offered me a last lingering glance with a wink that sent the same shivers through me as a frontal assault might, and then disappeared into the throng that filled Agarum's small lakefront. I deflated like a bellows, happy to be rid of her growing affections. She was cute in her own way and not much younger than me – she being nearly 16 and I nearly 18 – so there was nothing there for propriety's sake to prevent a match up. Around women, however, I was grossly immature having had little exposure to the desperate cultivations of teenage relationships. Oh, I'd asked girls out before – proms and such – with little success in formulating any true understanding of the opposite sex. As attractive as they were, I could not reach them on an emotional or intellectual level, and more often than not, they found my pale skinny frame, sunken chest, and wispy chin hair a laughable turn-off.

Jindan, however, was unlike any girl I had met before, mostly because she genuinely seemed to be attracted to me. This proved as intimidating as it was perplexing and it was further complicated by the fact that she'd spent several years as a child prostitute and had likely committed a murder or two as well. That was just plain terrifying – a more alien concept I couldn't grasp as I looked upon the elfin creature trotting away through the crowd. I mused a while longer, gulping like a fish in my anxiety. Then remembering the insult of being left alone while the *wallahs* were whisked away to our new castrum, I grew morose and stalked off the beach and into the crowded lakefront to find a watering hole to drown my sorrows and wait for a pickup.

Nearly a thousand people lived in Agarum – a confounding collection of refugees, adventurers, criminals, and the downtrodden – all out for a second chance on a new world. They had come from the refugee camps operated by United Nations in Afghanistan and Tajikistan as well as the Sudans and the Congo. Attracted by the offer of free land for settling, they left Earth in droves for the colony, and many had settled in Agarum to fish and farm, or to work the long hours in the supporting industries such as logging, shipbuilding, and road building. It was a hard existence in a cruel land, and they were often as poor as they had been in the refugee camps. On Samsāra, however, they owned land; two hectares per family. It meant farming and logging plots up and down the vallis and along the lakefront in the Seleucus Vallis proper as well. Most of the inhabitants of Agarum had farms that they tended during the summer. Half chose to return to the town for the brutal winter, living off their meagre profits while the other half stayed on their land year round in the vallis. The latter had an even harder existence as only a thin tenuous road through the mud connected the farmsteads and the sole centre of humanity within walking or riding distance.

I made my way from the crowded lakeshore where workers unloaded boxes and sacks from a docked paddlewheeler, and another group of impoverished, desperate men hired for an afternoon unloaded a new pre-fab habitation the size of a bus from another barge grounded on the beach. I pushed through narrow Dickensian streets of mud, manure, and sand, thick with crowds of every race and creed in creation, as I looked desperately for a place to shelter from the miserable drizzle that had begun. I finally found myself in a filthy public house built from a shipping container, the twin side doors swung open to reveal the diminutive bar inside and a few chairs and tables clustered around a wood stove.

It was inviting for the simple fact that it was dry with an illusion of warmth near the stove, so I sat down at a small round table stained deeply with beer rings and slopped food to enjoy the meagre heat from the stove while I sipped local rotgut whisky and generally felt sorry for myself. I had a few hours to kill and I found myself drawing out my compu-pad to ruminate on the video email I had received from my parents.

"Incredibly stupid," was the pronouncement from my mother delivered with the timbre of a Deadwood hanging judge when I finally worked up the nerve to inform her and my father of my fate, a mere week before as I sat maudlin in an Ophir bar and preparing to miss my first Christmas with my family in a couple of months. My father stared with cold disdain in the video before resuming the reading of his morning news with little more than a grunt of disgust.

I found their reactions rather puzzling – derision more than concern and hauteur over worry. I blame it on nothing more than an incomprehensible ignorance, for how could they have known, mere months before as they mused in disquieted anger that I had likely run off after some girl whom I'd met online, that I was actually splashing ashore from the ruin of a smoking paddlewheeler to forge up a rocky beach into a hellish maelstrom of gunfire from the Tongs of Coloe Vallis?

I continued to puzzle over their reaction during the days that followed. Vomiting and miserable as I was on the barge, I wondered what exactly they imagined I was doing on Samsāra, 20 light years from Earth? Did it mean anything to them? Did it register that their son was now months away beyond a hyperspace jump gate and fighting for his life against pirates, gangsters, aliens, and criminals? It hadn't, they told me years later. They thought it some foolish adventure – like joining the Boy Scouts or traveling as a groupie for a Roller Derby team. Just another flight of boyish fantasy and one that would be assuaged as it had been in my early teens by tramping about the woods for a few days, encountering the odd bear or two and then returning home hungry and in need of a bath. Well, it wasn't quite the same this time as there was every indication that I'd find a bullet long before I found the serenity they imagined I sought.

Yes, even now in my dotage, when I lounge in a hammock beneath the canopy of chestnut branches in my backyard and sip a crisp Riesling with notes of lime and peach from Oliver, British Columbia, or perhaps a Pinot Grigio from Kelowna – it matters not in the end – I wonder at my parents' reaction. They had assumed that I was in some camp, spending my hours in some silly manual labour or perhaps merely arts and crafts. Or that I had been wandering about the colony discovering new plants and animals, shivering in my sleeping bag in the evenings, and waking up late to a breakfast of waffles and scrambled eggs. Perhaps I was on the beach, they had thought, flirting with Amazonian university girls or strumming a guitar while friends stoked a campfire and we toasted the dawn with a fine Marchel Foch. Honestly, I'm not making this up; this is what passed through their minds when they discovered my fate. Never had I experienced such wide-eyed oblivious postulations, unless of course, I recall my own as I set foot in that hellish colony.

As my parents imagined me in a slow moving line for hotdogs and chips, I was eating cold *pilaf* and washing it down with brackish water. As they imagined me in a sleeping bag in some bunkhouse with a dozen other boys my age telling foolish stories into the wee hours, I was shivering in - 20^0 C in a small *hootchie* tent snuggled as close as I dared to my tent mate, Usman Khan – a sort of Artful Dodger with a 9mm Berretta and a Khyber knife. When they were sipping a Chardonnay and snacking on smoked salmon while overlooking Okanagan Lake and the distant Mount Nkwala, they imagined me playing team sports like softball and soccer. In reality I was fighting for my life in a trench with 50 other jawans, fighting hand-to-hand with a grey haired old Tong warrior whom I shot and killed. (The first of many kills I regretfully report.) It's hard to imagine my parents' assumptions and the reality of my new life in the Legion being further apart. As frivolous as my decision was to them, their gratuitous ignorance was its equal. Each time death stared me down, my parents imagined I was cooking Smores, canoeing, or just plain loafing about like a Senator in the Red Chamber.

I did love my parents even though I chose to break their hearts. Fleeing from their claustrophobic embrace and manipulative career goals to join the United Nations Off-World Legion was no act of malice, but in the months that followed my disappearance, I know for a fact they took it as such. No, aside from escaping their clingy grasp that sought to crush my personal aspirations, as baffling as they were at the time – I had had a real desire to work on trains, a horror to my white collar liberal vineyard owning parents who thought I'd make a fine journalist – my real aim was to see the frontier. That the frontier happened to be on Samsāra was a bonus that gave me extra time and distance from my old life which had become a drudgery. I know what you're thinking, "Old life, eh? At 17?" Well, true enough. I was a froward youth, and my stubborn streak combined with my naivety led me to believe that an existence on the frontier would be the culmination of all of my adventurous musings. Well it was that, and then some. Whether it was wading ashore on the beach of Coloe Vallis under the withering fire of 300 Black Hand gangsters or fleeing a handful of Narasimhan Indians after trying to pinch an adolescent prehistoric indricotherium that was to be raised and armed as a four legged tank, danger and adventure were constant companions. The fact that this was lost on my parents was never more apparent than during my first winter in Samsāra when, as the snows began to fall, my parents thought that at least I'd improve my skiing.

"You want another drink?" asked the barkeep as he sponged down my table with a rag that looked like it had been used to wipe down a sow, and then brought me over a bowl of steaming noodles. I nodded as I scooped in the scorching meal, the first I'd been able to choke down in two days. I fumbled with the chopsticks; I'd kept my wool fingerless gloves on against the chill, and then gratefully accepted the glass of whisky. It was rotten stuff, but it gave me warmth against the penetrating chill, and the noodles, spicy with real heat, were most welcome. I paid little heed to my surroundings as I ate, but my attention was wrenched as the chair beside me was pulled out and a slender, nuggety little man in a black battered Stetson took a seat opposite me.

"Don't you stop, hoss," he said as he chewed the stem of a short wooden pipe before pulling it out from beneath a massive greying moustache the size of a mongoose to tamp tobacco into it. "You're about as thin as a gnat's whisker, so you might had better get them noodles into ye."

My hand froze as I sat agog at the man before me. He slipped the pipe back in his mouth, lit it with a match scratched off the table, and leaned back in his chair until it touched the wall while placing a pair of faded cowboy boots thick with muck and manure on the table beside my bowl. It was hardly the Savoy Grill I'll admit, but I was horribly taken aback by the affront to my strict restaurant etiquette. I placed the chopsticks on the table and gently pushed the bowl away from me.

"I'm done," I announced.

"Are you now?" the man asked with some surprise as he lifted his Stetson off and placed it on the floor beside his chair. His was a balding pate with a comb over of greying stringy hair. "Well then," he puffed on his pipe and stuck out his hand, "we've howdied, but we ain't shook. Warden Tyrel Bohman, Pavonis Constabulary."

I couldn't shake the man's hand without standing, which I suspect was his plan all along. Seeing that this fellow was likely another colourful yet dangerous character of the frontier that I'd best not provoke, I stood, made my obedience, and introduced myself. "Jawan Alexander Armstrong, 9th Decuria, Panthera

Centuria, Ajax Legion," I rattled off formally, "but most call me Sikunder."

"Well now, Sikunder," Bohman replied from beneath a growing cloud of smoke. "Pleasure to be a-makin' your acquaintance. Yep, a real pleasure. Don't see many North Americans here 'bouts. As scarce as a virgin in a whorehouse they are. Where 'bouts you from?"

"Naramata, British Columbia."

"Western Canadian, are ye?" he said as his eyes widened in pleasure. They shrank back down to a bare squint as the cloud above him grew and he smiled – a wintry grimace beneath that magnificent moustache. "Well that's fine. Naramata, now, ain't that in Okanagan country?"

I nodded.

"I might oughta be a-makin' ye out as one of those citified dogies raised on concrete; normally the kind that couldn't hit a floor after fallin' out of the bed." He chuckled at his own wit while I reddened with embarrassment and anger. "That said, how long you been here?"

"Six months now."

"Six months, ye say?" Bohman said with some surprise as he signalled to the barkeep. "Well then, let's be a-puttin' the little pot into the big pot and have a drink to ye livin' that long!"

A moment later a pair of glasses appeared and Bohman raised his in a salute. "Here's to panties, hoss. Not the best thing in the world but damned close to it."

I nearly choked on the drink and a wide grin crossed Bohman's cadaverous face. "Easy there, hoss, don't need you drunk as Cooter Brown now. Just you be a-takin' it easy there. Now," he paused as he worked his pipe, "you a-bein' here six months and a-bein' one of MacShaka's squaddies," he said as he

19

pulled the pipe out of his mouth and pointed the chewed stem at my scarf, a brilliant red Royal Stewart tartan given to me by MacShaka to mark me as one of his decuria, "I'm a-guessin' you went in against the Tongs in the Coloe Vallis?"

I nodded and sipped my drink eager to see his reaction.

"Well that's interestin'. I a-figured you to be about as useful as a wheelbarrow with rope handles, but if you went in with MacShaka and that ol' devil MacGrogan-Singh, there just might could be more to ye."

It was about what I expected; he was yet another old warhorse eager to put a greenhorn such as myself in my place.

"Yep, that bein' said, maybe there's more to ye." He winked, sipped his whisky, and then added, "You come in with that herd of cattle?"

I nodded.

"Thought I saw you come in with that pack o' dogies all nosier than a cat makin' kittens. That she-devil, the little Hindu girl with a gap-tooth grin, the one as pretty as twelve acres of pregnant hotdogs, now she looked like she was about as handy as shirt pockets. Got the feelin' she was liketa runnin' that show." He smiled slyly.

"Maybe. It was my first time working with cattle," I replied while looking away and feeling embarrassed.

"Ah yes, I was a-thinkin' that much."

There was a pause as he sipped his drink and I decided it was my turn to ask some questions.

"How long have you been Warden here?"

"Well now, hoss," he replied as he signalled for another round, "I been out here for about 10 years now. Ain't that odd? I'm a-thinkin' I'm a few pickles short of a barrel at times. Been out here long enough that friends back home think I don't know a widget from a whangdoodle now."

"And where is home?"

"Hell, hoss, that's Texas; little place called Eden, half way between Austin and Abilene, town no bigger than moles on a chigger. I was working near Houston when I came out here though; was a Texas Ranger when I decided to put out the fire and call in the dogs. Head out to the frontier, I told my friends." He took the newly arrived drink and took a long sip. "Ain't never looked back."

"You were a Texas Ranger?" I asked as I burst through any level of caution, and aimed my foot right for my mouth. "What, kind of like the Lone Ranger?"

Bohman squinted more, if that was at all possible, and looked at me as if I'd farted. "Lick the calf again?" he asked as he gave me a searching gaze. "Hell, hoss, you could screw up an anvil with thinkin' like that. No wonder MacShaka put the she-dogie in charge. MacShaka might outghta tie a quarter to ye and throw it away, At least he could say he lost something then." This was delivered with a grin that made the crow's feet of his eyes deepen followed by a dry chuckle.

Well, that was me, put squarely in my place. What a curious fellow this one was, all friendly hillbilly and deadly Wyatt Earp. He ran his hand over his balding head, and his black mud-spattered duster fell away revealing a faded sheriff's badge on his black *sherwani* coat beneath the crossed bandoliers of 45 calibre bullets for his pistol. He also wore the black *salwars* of the Constabulary, an odd contrast to the cowboy duster and Stetson, but that was Tyrel Bohman, one of the many curious fixtures of the frontier.

"Tell ye what, hoss," he said as he dropped his feet to the floor and slowly stood up. "You look like you was born tired and since had a relapse. Plus, you're still so skinny ye'd have to stand twice to make a shadow. Let's go to a place I know for a good meal."

As much as I was feeling a bit of caution, the man was the Warden of the Constabulary in Aebbas Vallis, so I figured it was safe enough. I was a bit tipsy as I rose to my feet, and putting my *Pakol* beret on my head and shouldering my pack, I followed Bohman out the door and into the muck of the street.

"Well now, I oughta could use a cup of coffee; coffee so strong as to go a-walkin into my cup. Then a steak, I'm a-thinkin'. How's about you, hoss?"

"Steak's fine," I replied with a bit of slur. Bohman grinned.

"Come along then."

Bohman led the way, his diminutive figure stalking through the malodorous mess of the narrow streets, pushing through the jabbering throng that, for the most part, dissipated away from him. Once in a while we'd be caught in the crowd, usually a group of lost settlers trying to set themselves up for the move to a homestead in the vallis, and he'd wade into them with a Texas-sized tantrum.

"Ya'll git outta my way. Hell, anytime any of ye are a-passin' my house, just you keep on a-going'! Watch your step, ye addle-headed barber's cats! If you was bacon ya wouldn't even sizzle!"

These were all delivered with that grimacing smile of his and a hand resting on the grip of his heavy pistol. The streets cleared, even of tundra camels and a solitary mastodon loaded with tents and packs as it and its harried *mahout* and a score of Chinese settlers prepared to move inland. Finally we rounded a corner, and a small rough-hewn building appeared tucked between of dilapidated yurts. The entrance was crowded with filthy refugees and settlers standing around with bowls of noodles and rice, but

Bohman pushed through to enter the hellish funk within. "Come on, hoss, it ain't so bad once ya get used to it. It's hotter than a summer revival and the owner looks like she sorts bobcats for a livin', but they cook a mean steak."

It was standing room only in that sweltering Bedlam and I wondered how we could possibly find a place to sit when I spied an empty table in the corner near the stove – oddly empty given the jostling crowd around it. Bohman headed right for it, and I quickly figured that this was his private table, for within moments of sitting down a grizzled Chinese woman with piled grey hair held in place with hairsticks and wearing a filthy apron appeared.

"Wa'den," she said, thin-lipped and serious as she bowed. "You hea' fo' coffee?"

"I sure am," Bohman said with that friendly grin, "and not any of that belly wash you serve to the local bushwhackers either, Su Li-ya. I want coffee so strong it'll raise a blood blister on my boot. My chickabiddy friend here," he said as he pointed the stem of his pipe at me, "will be a-takin' a cup as well. Then we'll be a-havin' some chow, a couple of beefsteaks. Beefsteaks, I'm a-sayin', Li-ya, and none of that crowbait horse you feed the masses, either."

The owner disappeared, and Bohman moved his chair close to me, leaned back, and placed his boots on the table. "Now that's a might warmer, hoss. Hell, warmer than whoopee in woollens," he added with a chuckle. He took his hat off and said in a raised voice, "When I came to Agarum two years ago, this village was nothin' more than a few dozen stumps, and this here cabin. Looked like Hell with everyone out to lunch. Surrounded by nothing more than blue UN issue tents and few yurts it was, but the chow was good; can't beat that with a stick these days. That or you're eatin' UN fixin's – the worst kind; pre-packaged food made in Bulgaria or some such place – nothin' to write home about. This place though, ain't bad. "

The coffee arrived – hot and strong – and it cut through the sluggishness from the whisky.

"Now that's coffee, hoss," he said with a wink. "There was many a day I'd have given my right arm for a fair to middlin' cup of Joe in the early days. Hell, in Ophir I could get it, but Ophir was just too damned big. Figured I might oughta come here for the quiet when the UN opened this here vallis for settlin'."

"That's why you're here?" I asked. Bohman nodded.

"Sure is. Quiet country two years ago; handful of families, store, this here little cantina, and some prospectors. Look at the place now though; 1,000 people in this town if'n there's one. Further up the vallis, 'nother 1,000 or so. All greenhorn prospectors and settlers tryin' to shake out a livin' in the mud." He pointed the stem of his pipe east. "One muddy little road, thin as store bought thread, runs the length of the vallis; from Agarum 10 klicks east to your new castrum, Sommerkveld. They're a-buildin' it at the confluence of the Aebbas Fluman and the Ceallach, by the way, right beside the bridge that crosses from Aebbas Sultus to Gleann Ceallach. Gonna be a real treat for you to watch that, hoss," he said with a guffaw. "Yep, y'all be as busy as a stump-tailed bull in fly season!" he added as he slapped the table and laughed.

I wasn't sure what he was referring to, having only just arrived and not having the benefit of the decuria's two previous weeks in the vallis. I queried his meaning and he winked.

"It's like this, hoss," he said after a pull from his mug. "There are about 2,000 settlers in Aebbas Vallis; scores more come in every month. UN sends refugees here faster than a sneeze through a screen door now that Ophir is near full. Now you see here, hoss,

24

Ilken Vallis, just north of Ophir, is full of those Neo Cossacks, and they're meaner than a mama wasp; no UN refugees a-goin' there. Geordan Vallis, north of them, they'd steal your mama's egg money, but the UN can get a couple score of refugees in there each month. Mind, more'n likely they'll all be she-bears in satin a year from now. Bryna Vallis, north of those folks, well, hoss, they're a might more crooked than a dog's leg in there, and the Constabulary has got to slop the hogs, dig the well, and plow the south forty before breakfast, but it's a long vallis and the UN can get a thousand refugees in there a year. We're next up here; they need to be a-fillin' us up before they move north to Maximan Vallis to the east, though that place has a couple thousand in there already. Figure we can take about another thousand or more, give 'em land and hope to terrace the sides of the vallis before we put up the full sign. Problem is, they're a-leakin' into Gleann Ceallach. Might oughta go from a leak to a gusher if we ain't careful."

"What's the problem with that?" I asked. It seemed normal — overflow from the vallis into Gleann Ceallach, a much larger 35 kilometre long valley to the east that ran north/south. I said as much, which elicited an ironic laugh from Bohman.

"You'd think that, hoss," he said as he waved at the barkeep. "Problem is there ain't no law in there. Place is filled with varmints so low you couldn't put a rug under them; gangs, and them varmints the *Chúsheng*, all a-fightin' with each other and the settlers and all of them killin' any lawman who crosses their border with Aebbas Vallis. Even got a few hundred Gliesiuns in there rootin' in the muck. Hell, in my two years here, I've lost seven constables in there. Lost a dozen in here too," he added as he slapped the table. "We got enough lawbreakers this side of the Ceallach. Lately though, them folk been crossin' the Ceallach and causin' me grief.

That's why they decided to build a castrum on the border and put you squaddies in here."

"Remind me again what exactly the *Chúsheng* are?" I'd heard the term bantered about in my brief time here, and all that I knew is that were generally considered criminals.

"Hell, hoss, you been here six months and no one has explained the *Chúsheng* to you?" He looked at me askance and shrugged. "Pretty easy really. They're settlers who didn't make it at farming and turned to stealing instead. Most are pretty tame; they raid food mostly and sometimes cattle. Others, well, hoss, they're mean; mean enough to jump on you with all four feet. Killers they are. My constables can usually deal with them, but if'n they get big numbers, well, that's when you squaddies oughta mighta weigh in," he finished with a wink.

So, that was it. I had briefly wondered at the reason for building a new castrum deep in the vallis. I hadn't had the chance to find out before I was bundled off to herd cattle, but I had assumed it was just another normal event in the colony. It was anything but. The UN didn't have a good picture of just how many refugees and settlers had moved into Gleann Ceallach, nor any idea how many Gliesiuns had trickled in over the years. Building a castrum and placing 50 or more jawans at the border between the two suggested there was a real problem though, and that my chances of survival were going to take a turn for the worse.

The barkeep arrived with our steaks and followed them up with two glasses of whisky. Bohman ate with enthusiasm, voraciously shoving the barely cooked meat into his mouth with the rapidity of a starving man. It took him no more than five minutes to clean his plate, which meant he could again sit back, rest his boots on the table, and reload his pipe.

I resisted the urge to push my plate away this time for I was truly famished. I ate my steak, undercooked as it was and lacking the accompaniment of a fine merlot, and drank back the whisky. The plates vanished and Bohman watched the crowd in silent contemplation. "These folks here, hoss," he said after a long pause, "they ain't got nowhere else to go. If the UN can't find room for them, and it's filling up faster in here than a prairie fire with a tail wind, then they'll go into Gleann Ceallach. Problem is, eventually someone will have to be a-goin' in there to sort them out. I don't want to be the gump who has to go in there pistols blazin'."

"Go in there?" I asked after downing my whisky, for his tough talk was giving me a case of the willies. "What would you go in there for?"

"Hell, hoss," he replied as he waved to the bartender. "I'm a-bettin' by the spring, what with the vallis bein' as busy as a funeral home fan in July, that the UN'll be openin' Gleann Ceallach for settlin'. Gonna be a hell of a mess to clean up when the settlers start goin' in full force. Likely it'll be the Legion leadin' that charge," he added with a cackle.

"The Legion isn't supposed to fight settlers," I countered, though without much conviction. "We're supposed to stand between the Terrans and Gliesiuns."

"Is that the case?" Bohman fired back with a glint in his eye. "How 'bout them Tongs ya'll put down six months ago. Or the Kazakhs a few years back in Ilken Vallis? Think the Legion must have forgotten their mandate, eh? "

I was full on worried by now, and when he looked at me slantendicular for a few moments, I knew instantly that he recognized that. His wintry smile appeared and he slapped the table again.

"Whether the Legion or the Company like it or not, hoss, they're the powerhouse in this here colony. The Constabulary ain't got the firepower to deal with anything beyond petty thugs and small time gangs. Organizations like the Black Hand have to fall under the purview of the Legion. Come the spring, when the UN opens up Gleann Ceallach to formal settlement, there'll be Gliesiuns and *Chúsheng* already well established and waiting for new victims to come in. The 20 Constables I have on the border wouldn't last a day. The Legion on the other hand, hell, they'll have to ride point and maybe hoss, just maybe, we avoid a lotta blood being spilt."

My shoulders slumped in defeat. In only a few frigid months, I'd be back at it again, wondering when my parents would receive that message of condolence because their son had been picked off in a valley whose name no one could even pronounce without losing a litre of phlegm. Bohman looked upon me and his craggy face softened a trifle.

"How's about I give you a ride to the castrum, hoss. Even though you've been a-shootin' your mouth off so much ye must eat bullets for breakfast, I figure I can put up with yer company a bit longer. Save ya jawin' poor Li-ya to her grave."

I couldn't say no, for I was beginning to long for a proper bed after so much beef and whisky, and although the prospect of 10 kilometres of rutted trail didn't thrill me, I'd rather get it done now than wait for that cranky naique to decide to return.

"Come on then," he said as he plopped his Stetson on his head and stood up. "Office is just a couple of blocks away."

Bohman led me through the throng, and I was fascinated that the table remained empty after we left. It was a testament to the power of this man, not only to the authority of the law that the UN hired him to uphold, but to the strength of a personality that could so dominate the people around him. He wasn't much to look at, save for the massive moustache and the cold grey eyes, and yet men much larger and as well armed melted before him like butter in a desert. It was captivating to watch – the bows, curtsies, *salaams*, dropped eyes, and even ham-handed salutes – as Bohman led me through the crowd. If some unknowing stranger neglected to show respect, Bohman unleashed no end of Texan invective, with a smile on his face and a hand on his pistol. When one hulking Sikh, filthy from days on the long muddy trail up the east side of the vallis from Ophir, glared disdainfully at Bohman's, "You smell like you want to be left alone. Now get out of the way!" the bantam warden swung a clenched fist with the rapidity of a machine gun until the giant lay crying in the mud. "Get up now, hay seed, and move along," he said as he helped the staggering man to his feet, dabbed at the open cut on the Sikh's eyebrow, twisted his broken nose back into place, and then gave him an apple from the pocket of his duster before pushing him along.

"Tell ye what, hoss, that big buck there is dumb enough for twins, but I might oughta have to look him up later and see if'n he'd join the Constabulary. Big and dumb sometimes comes in handy."

Bohman chuckled to himself for a few moments until a scream emanated from around the corner. His hand dropped to his pistol and he strode off on his diminutive legs while I loped along behind. He pushed through a wall of jabbering refugees all smelling of *ghee* oil and garlic until we stood in an open circle surround by a wall of wide-eyed witnesses. In the centre lay a diminutive Chinese refugee, his throat slit wide open with blood pooling below his neck. Beside him knelt his wife holding a baby, shrieking in horror as the man's eyes dimmed in death. She was keening and wailing, pounding the mud while above her stood a towering Pashtun, all dyed red beard and menacing as he held a bloody Khyber knife and a small cloth bag.

His hand still resting on his pistol, Bohman waited for the cacophony of the crowd to subside as it did in a few moments, leaving an eerie silence as that Texas David looked upon the Goliath of the Hindu Kush.

"Well now, Hakim Sulumani, what's a-goin' on here?" Bohman asked with an icy calm.

Sulumani smiled, panting heavily in his excitement of bloodletting, and pointed his bloody knife towards the corpse at his feet. "*Bismillah*, this *wald il qahbaa* stole from me! At *fāntān*!" He held up the cloth bag. "Thirty grams of gold and he cheated me out of it, and when I tried to get it back, he said he would kill me for it, *La ilaha illa Allah*."

Bohman kept his eyes on him. "That little feller, there, the one about as half as big as a minute? He said he'd kill you now? And that's scared ya silly enough to cut his throat?"

"He said he had a knife," Sulumani replied. "He might have stabbed me."

"And you with that Arkansas toothpick," Bohman replied evenly. "You should oughta be a-droppin' that right about now, Hakim, by the way."

Sulumani stood tall, puffed his chest, raised the knife, and eyed Bohman with a basilisk's stare.

"I will do no such thing, *Bismillah*."

"It'd be best if'n ya did that, Hakim." Bohman tapped his pistol with a finger.

"Yamin Atayev will not be happy with that, you *bin'nt himaar*!" he replied with a dangerous glint.

"That's some sweet talk, ye got there, Hakim. Lord willing and the creek don't rise, you'll be droppin' that pig sticker now though."

Sulumani continued to bristle. "I will not."

In a heartbeat there was a flash of movement, a click, the whine of a pistol powering up, and then a 'snap' as Bohman squeezed the rigger. Sulumani's head jerked backwards amidst a spray of crimson and he sank to his knees with a hole in his forehead. His eyes rolled up and he fell forward into the mud. Bohman tapped a comm link in his ear.

"Manute, this is Bohman. Come meet me by Chung's *Fāntān* House."

Bohman holstered his pistol and pulled out his pipe. I stared at the corpse of the hulking Pashtun, and then at the shrieking refugee. My heart was pounding and sweat was pouring down my back. I couldn't believe what I had just witnessed.

"Well," Bohman said as he lit his pipe. "That ain't gonna go over well. Yamin Atayev's a-goin' to pitch a fit over that sore arsed mush head."

"Who the hell is Yamin Atayev?" I asked. I fought hard to control my racing breathing.

"Yamin Atayev is one of the local pimps. Has a little gang of bravos into petty crime and the occasional murder." He sighed. "Had an understanding with the little pecker that I wouldn't kill his bulldog if'n he kept him under control. He didn't and now that bulldog is dead."

A powerful African in Constabulary garb arrived with a few others trailing behind. As the crowd began to disperse, Bohman explained the situation and moments later, the bodies and the grieving woman and her baby were cleared from the muck.

"Have to file a damned report on that," Bohman groused as he led me to the station a couple of blocks away. There I spied a battered Jeep that he pointed to. "Throw yer kit in the back and hop in."

It was 10 kilometres to the castrum on a road that was little wider than the jeep and rougher than a creek bed. The drizzle had stopped by this time, leaving the road slick with mud. Aebbas Vallis stretched out before us, darkened and damp beneath the glowering gloom. From either side of the road stretched out the homesteads – each a rectangle of land piled two or three high up the gentle rounded sides of the valley wall – long cleared of trees and now terraced and holding houses and outbuildings, and most with crops ready for harvesting. One could also see no end of cattle, goats, sheep, and pigs right up to the edge of the vallis's cultivated land. Beyond that, the trees resumed in a tall foreboding belt before fading to the cliff face and ridge tops high above. It was a romantic pastoral setting in some ways though the place reeked of poverty. The buildings were rough-hewn tumble-down affairs likely as not packed to the rafters with several generations of family. It was a damned sight better than the UN tent cities they had left in Afghanistan years before, I had to remind myself, each time some new vision of squalor met my eyes.

Bohman was a skilled driver as we bounced, rocked, and slid over that hellish track and he kept the vehicle moving and generally on course with little invective. There were plenty of stops of course, for horses, tundra camels, wagons, pedestrians, and creatures of every kind that were frequent users of this single track. He finally lost his temper though when a trio of *mahouts* couldn't control their mammoth, a four meter tall creature loaded down with rough cut planks and beams for delivery to some homestead. As the creature stood stubborn and irascible, its long russet locks thick with mud, it glared balefully while the *mahouts* whipped it, pleaded with it, and gnashed their teeth in frustration. Bohman looked on for a few moments and then exited the jeep in a fine fit of pique.

"Damn animal is so thick-headed you can hit it in the face with a tire iron and it won't yell till morning." To the drivers he snapped. "You three, move the damned animal or I'll do it for ya!"

"*Sahib*," said the lead *mahout* as he fawned with clasped hands, "the creature will not move."

"Yeah, I gathered that, ya damned chucklehead." Bohman pushed his Stetson back and spat. "I ain't got all day, there Brahma. You move him, or I will."

"*Sahib*," the *mahout* pleaded, "it will not move. You must wait."

"Well, you may have a yellow jacket in the outhouse, Brahma, and that's a fact, but I ain't got time for you to find the swatter." With that, he pulled out his pistol, powered it up, and loosed off a shot at the mammoth's massive head, nicking the creature's ear. The mammoth grunted, trumpeted in rage, and shambled off the road with the *mahouts* shrieking behind it. Bohman chuckled, spat again, and tossed his head towards the jeep. "Let's go, hoss. We're hollerin' down a well right now."

We arrived at Sommerkeld Castrum an hour later. The fort was under construction at the confluence of the Aebbas Flumen and the Ceallach, both narrow roaring cataracts that connected at the narrowing of the two valleys. Here, the walls of the vallis were much closer; powerful shoulders pushing together leaving only a narrow strip of usable land. The Constabulary had put a small detachment there a year ago after a bridge had been built across the Ceallach – now the castrum had come increasing the armed presence to nearly 80 rifles.

Bohman pulled the jeep up to the gate. "Alright, hoss, as much as I want to get out and share a bottle with MacShaka, I've got paperwork to do. So I'll drop you off and be a-gettin' back before dark."

I thanked him, grabbed my pack, and watched as he waved and turned the jeep around for his trip back. He was a fascinating character and one I was going to get to know much better in the coming months.

Part Three
Sommerkveld Castrum

Sommerkveld Castrum was definitely a going concern, or at least it was trying to be. Measuring some 100 meters squared on a flat patch of bog near the narrow bridge crossing the Ceallach, it contained rows of tents for each of the four contubernium – a section of 10 jawan soldiers – on its manicured muddy *maidan* as well as a larger mess tent, operations tent, stores containers, medical tent, garage, and stables. At each of the four corners stood a low, rough tower constructed of reused, rusting, shipping containers. The gabion walls and fascines of brushwood were still under construction, and what a lengthy process that appeared to be. Piles of sandbags were deposited around the perimeter for the jawans to stack into the empty wire gabion boxes which would eventually be three layers high for a total height of nearly three meters – just like Ophir Castrum's gabion walls – and high enough to keep out the worst of any trouble.

The gates were open now and guarded by a single jawan with a rifle who was smoking a cigar while looking positively bored. Affecting a nonchalance that was laughable amidst the gangs of filthy jawans who looked upon my arrival with humour (they all knew by now that I was late because the *wallahs* had been picked up first), I pulled down my Pakol beret over my brow while whistling Garry Owen, then strolled in to face the torment.

"Sikunder!" exclaimed my particular friend Usman Khan; he was a 16 year old roughneck from the refugee camps in Afghanistan who had taken to me as a boy to a puppy upon our arrival six months before. "You are back!" he said as he skipped up to me through the muck with a smile and an embrace. He was filthy with tundra camel dung and the smell was atrocious. "Come, drop your bag off and help me with the stables."

Well, a more alluring invitation I couldn't think of, and even as I made to shy off, our contubernium naique, a miserable retired mullah named Muneer Al-Shahid-Mahmood strode up wagging his finger at me. "Sikunder!" he roared all bristling and indignant, "Why is it you are always the last? *Bismillah*! The children are here, and yet you cannot show the same devotion to your duties?" He stood before me, hands on hips with eyes boring into me. Usman was smiling, which only earned him a swat on the back of the head from Muneer and an "Away with you, *maftooha*," which was pretty damned insulting if you ask me. Usman, however, shrugged it off, winked and ran back to the stables. "You may join him, jawan," Muneer said as he grabbed me by the ear – a painful and embarrassing tool of his that elicited no end of guffaws from the jawans around me – and deposited me in our contubernium tent. "Change and off to the stables."

It was the reception I had expected, though he seemed to be carrying it off a trifle high. I found out why during the hour I spent with Usman mucking out the stables, however.

"It is very dangerous here, Sikunder," Usman said as he brushed tundra camel dung off of his chin. "Across the river, in Gleann Ceallach, we get shot at."

"Shot at?" I asked as I paused to lean on my rake. I retched, fought back the bile from the atrocious smell one could almost taste, then asked, "Who the hell is shooting at us?"

"*Chúsheng*, they are called by the *huzúras*," Usman replied, lacking some of the impish humour that often marked him. "These particular creatures are animals, Sikunder, who live by preying on others." Usman glanced around as if afraid that one of the villains would suddenly pop out from behind the mounds of dung. "For the last two weeks we have been haunted by them. They shoot day and night but we have been fortunate, *dost*, for no one has been badly hit. Only the fat Hindu, Maddukuri, in Cong's contubernium was hit in his big belly!" Usman guffawed. "The woven armour of his *sherwani* and his fat saved him!"

This confirmed the brief account that Bohman had passed onto me; and if the descriptions I was to hear over the next few hours was any indication, these lawless, broken people, bereft of land and hope, were a horrific terror in the gleann and one that took great pleasure in poking the hornet's nest of the decuria's new castrum. In the two weeks that the decuria had been there, they had come under sporadic if ineffectual fire, suffering only the fat Hindu as a casualty. They had poured out time and again to chase the villains off, killing the occasional one only to have them sneak through the thick verdant undergrowth of Gleann Ceallach's flanks a day or two later. It was one of the disadvantages of our new position – built squarely in the centre of the vallis floor with at least 200 meters on either side of our walls – we were well situated to monitor the crossing of the Ceallach and its sole bridge, but with the tree line only 300 meters to the east, we had also placed ourselves in an ideal location to be well within range of snipers. The situation was compounded by the heavy foliage and rocky terrain, which provided great cover and ensured that our sensors had difficulty penetrating the gloom. Oh we were fortunate on occasion when someone blundered into the open long enough for our own snipers to take a crack at them, but those were rare opportunities. Luck had been with us so far, for the *Chúsheng* only seemed interested in mild harassment.

"Each day some of our work parties build the walls while others go out to thin the plants," Usman said as he sat on a bale of straw. "Twice now we have come across the *Chúsheng* and twice now they have retreated with fewer numbers. I even hit one with my rifle, *dost*!" he added with growing excitement. "To a true man, his sickle is a Khyber knife!"

"Aren't you clever," I replied a little sickened at his enthusiasm for bloodshed. I was being a bit unfair though, for he'd been there for the last two weeks while I had not. Our time in Ophir Castrum had been a paradise compared to this dreary place. Life in a castrum on open tundra with few visitors and most of them friendly drovers, and only a few hours to the town of Ophir and its many amenities had been pleasant. Here though, we were nearly on the frontier, hemmed in by the towering sylvan walls of the vallis and with only the mephitic dinginess of Agarum to fall back on.

"It is said that in a few days we may go and clear out the gleann in the south, but that came from Muneer, and he has been most unhappy lately."

"Hard to imagine," I groused as I slopped the muck. "What's his problem?"

"Desertion, *dost*," Usman replied, his dung smeared visage growing grim. "In our two weeks, three jawans have fled. None from our contubernium, but the naiques and havildars are most displeased."

"Desertion?" I replied. I'd heard of it of course, as it was hardly new to those decurias deployed to the more violent, remote, and hopeless regions in the colony. It usually occurred most often in the far north, so I was rather taken aback that we had lost three of our numbers in such a short period of time. "There is always talk now," Usman continued. "In the shadows, jawans speak of fleeing. Some talk of going into Gleann Ceallach to the villages there where they feel the Legion might not follow to look for them. Some talk of going north while some even talk of going far to the south to the Leman Campus."

"I just came from there," I replied. "There's not much to go to.'

'They don't know that, *dost*," Usman said. "They are afraid. Ahk, cowards! We need to go out and fight!" He mucked about for a few moments before he added, "All of this is harder because along with the *Chúsheng*, we still have the settlers and traders who cross the Ceallach every day. And then there are the Gliesiuns." He paused and laid his doe eyes on me. "We do not know what they will do."

It was all hopelessly complicated really, a Machiavellian shambles that made the chaos of the UN refugee camps in Afghanistan appear well ordered in comparison. I didn't muse on it long, however, for I'd long since ceased being surprised by the sometimes feudal nature of this curious colonial experiment. Most of the citizens who made up the population of Samsāra knew no better existence, and in truth, I doubt it would have been much different had the majority been Scots, Swedes or Canadians instead of Chinese, Pashtuns and Kazakhs. Mind, hockey and curling would have been a delight to watch.

When we had finished for the afternoon and sprinted from the shower tent wrapped only in towels through a drizzle turning rapidly to sleet as the temperature dropped for the evening, I was confronted with perhaps the most terrifying scene I had witnessed so far. As Usman and I pushed into the contubernium tent I stopped short, for there, sitting on the cot beside mine, was Jindan. Her gap-toothed smile widened and she said most welcomingly, "*Namastē, Sirdar*," as she stood and brought her hands together in a bow.

I pulled my towel closer and took a step back.

"What are you doing here?" I asked.

"I live here now, *Sirdar*," she replied with a wink. She patted her cot. "Right here, beside you." She stood ramrod straight and saluted. "Jawan Jindan Chandrakala, 9th Decuria, Panthera Centuria, Ajax Legion, *Sirdar*!"

Usman elbowed me in the ribs and laughed. The rest of the contubernium were there: Muneer Al-Shahid-Mahmood who lay dozing on his cot; Yee Hong-miao and Fung Wai-ting – two 16 year old Han Chinese as pale as porcelain dolls who were busy braiding each other's long hair; the mercurial old Greek fisherman, Lukianos Kondylis, who was trimming his white beard with a pair of tiny brass scissors; and Makemba Adoula and Amina Barre – one a female Congolese freedom fighter and the other a shy Ethiopian lass – who sat playing a clapping game called *Tobeta Maboko*. Yes, they were all there, and each paused in their activities to stare at me. Not Muneer though, he simply began to snore.

"Uh," I found myself stumbling over my words. How could this be? I wondered in horror. She was 15 and a *wallah* – an underage non combatant in the Legion. Yes, we were short a jawan since the death of Yang Zhi-hong, the third of our 16 year old Chinese girls, on the beach of the Coloe Vallis five months before, but this was so wrong. She was still a child soldier in the Legion's very ethically bankrupt definition, not 16 years old.

The tent door opened behind me and our contubernium havildar entered, a plumpish motherly type named Sittana Kayra. She was a jolly Sudanese, a woman whom I rather liked as she was usually fair, hit me rarely, and did what she could to make my generally miserable existence just a bit more tolerable.

"Sikunder," she said with a smile that revealed a mouthful of brilliant white teeth. "You've decided to rejoin us have you?" She gave me a mild push towards my cot. "Don't stand in the entrance."

Jindan made room for me to stumble towards my cot and foot locker. I held my towel tighter while she slowly sat on her cot, her eyes holding mine.

"Uh," I looked at Sittina. "Uh, havildar," I asked with a pathetic stage whisper, "what's she doing here?"

Sittina sat on her cot and sleeping bag and unlaced her boots. "Sikunder, I do hope you wished Jawan Chandrakala a happy birthday on your mission. She turned 16, you know."

I snapped my head to stare at the impish girl who smiled and gave me the prettiest little wave. To think only nine days before she'd been calling for slit throats amongst the Black Hand bandittos who had lifted our herd of cattle.

"Nnn, no," I stammered. I was buffaloed. I hadn't heard a thing about this. I spared Usman a furious glance – the damned rascal had known all along while we were mucking out the stables. While the remainder of the contubernium grinned at my obvious discomfort, Jindan only shrugged.

"The *Sirdar* was very busy, *Sahiba*," she said. "I did not wish to bother him."

"And," Sittina said as she laid down on her cot for a pre-supper nap, "we're still a jawan short. So now we have Jawan Chandrakala joining our contubernium."

It took some effort to dress myself beneath that towel while Chandrakala stared upon me with obvious feeling. What she saw in me – a 17 year old dropout from high school with downy fuzz on my chin; a pale, sunken chest; little more than toothpicks for arms and legs; a tenor voice at best; and moon eyes like a child, my mother said – was far beyond me. It wasn't that I didn't think she was cute in a sword-wielding, throat cutting, Boadicea sort-of-way, but I continued to find her obvious affection unreasonably frightening and it hurled me into adolescent angst and a torpor of self consciousness. So here, on Samsāra, so far from home, the starry-eyed pining of a 16 year old girl who'd likely killed more men than a Pashtu horse thief truly threw me off my pace.

Once dressed I lay down on my cot, draped my Pakol beret over my eyes and shammed sleeping in order to give myself pause to think; it would only be a matter of time before I would be called to order by Jindan, and the thought of her and her Khyber knife was enough to give me the fearful hiccups.

That quickly foiled my fake somnolence.

"You are not sleeping, *Sirdar*," Jindan said in her sing-song voice.

I whipped off my Pakol and sat up. Looking around to ensure that no one in the tent was outwardly eavesdropping, I leaned towards her and whispered through clenched teeth, "It ain't right, you eyeing me like that. It makes me feel," I paused to consider which word would save me a gutting, "uncomfortable."

"I understand," Jindan said with a smile. "You are shy. That is fine, *Sirdar*. I do not think you will be shy forever though. It is said, *Who saw a peacock dance in the woods?*"

"What?" I hissed. Why did every creature in creation think I should understand their nonsensical idioms and proverbs?

"Someday, Sikunder, all will know of your feelings."

Fat chance of that, I thought as my hand went to my stomach. She'd be unsheathing her Khyber knife and playing Pinfinger with my spleen if she knew the truth. The best, and healthiest option, was to play the shy jawan for now to give myself time to figure a way out of my predicament.

"Uh, sure." That ineffectual response didn't seem to bother her as she lay down on her sleeping bag and spared me a wink before closing her eyes for a nap. I exhaled softly.

"Oh dear."

* * * * *

"Sikunder, ye glumshie greetin' faced cuddie! I see ye hae decided tae join the land o' the livin' instead of moochin' about the tundra chasin' coos!"

This was the greeting after a fashion, given by our decuria subedar, Angus Motshegwa, more affectionately referred to as MacShaka the Tartan Zulu. The fact that it was also delivered a meter behind me at the volume of a bear roaring after a hornet sting on the balls made me fumble my food tray and nearly pee myself in terror. I spun around after picking up my tray to view the monster as he towered above me – all Cetshwayo and MacIain of Glencoe mixed into a stew of hot Celtic blood and Zulu intransigence. He stood before me, hands on hips, his long sable beard braided into forks and falling down his cobalt blue *sherwani* to the belt of his scarlet *salwars*. His bald head was bare, and most unusual for him, there was the vaguest hint of amusement in his deep brooding eyes.

"And here I thought ye was far through after I heard tell o' ye drinkin' wi' that auld yin, Bohman. Well on were ye when he drew on that torn-faced draigled puddock,   Hakim Sulumani?"

"I'm not sure," I said, picking out only a few words of what he'd said. There were times like now when I thought much of his hideous brogue was put on for my benefit. I never worked up the nerve to ask, mind.

"Make no never mind," MacShaka said as he clapped me on the arm and sent my tray to the ground again. "Losh, Sikunder," he said over the laughs, "ye wee bauchle. Away wi' ye and eat before ye fall down."

Red faced, I received my meal of *pilaf* and overcooked goat, and found a spot in the far corner away from the general noisy hubbub of the supping decuria. Usman soon joined me as did Jindan, much to my discomfort. Sittina was the last of our cozy foursome, and I dug in with gusto having two days of seasickness to recover from. Jindan ate slowly, eyeing me and smiling while Usman looked between us and laughed while muttering some unkind quips in Pashto. Sittina said nothing for a while, opting to cuff Usman for his bad manners, and then remarked, "I would guess Jawan Khan here has given you the layout of our new home and its situation?"

"Kind of," I replied. I gave her the précis that Usman had shared – the *Chúsheng*, the sniping, the traffic of settlers and traders, and the Gliesiuns.

"That covers a lot of it," Sittina said with a nod. She licked her fingers before adding, "A few more facts for you to know though. Gleann Ceallach is a unique place being an unofficial settlement with maybe, 1,000 people in it right now. Most of those folks are simply poor settlers who, disliking their land plots in Aebbas Vallis or Bryn Vallis to the south, opted to move into the glean where they could claim larger plots."

"How do they do that?" I interrupted. Sittina spared me a withering glance.

"Not all of the trees in the forest make good firewood it seems," she replied with a hint of annoyance. I knew when to shut up, even if it sometimes came after the fact. "When the UN puts up land for settlement, each individual plot is two hectares or 200 meters squared. That's what each family gets. That's alright for a small family, but a larger family, with more children who may want to divide it in future, will find two hectares too small. They can compete for another couple of hectares, but with the number of settlers the UN is pushing in here and the slowness to open and develop land, they won't get it. So that leaves the settlers only a few options. Buy up land adjacent to theirs, buy up land in the same vallis or in another vallis, or push their way into a vallis that has not yet been put up for settlement."

"That's seems like a no brainer," I said.

"You'd think," Sittina said with just enough sarcasm for me to redden. "You've only seen the valles that have been developed, Sikunder," she said before pushing her bowl back and reaching for her demitasse of coffee.

Developed, I thought. If I'd only seen the developed settlements then I shuddered to think what undeveloped looked like.

"Any settler can go into undeveloped land. No development means no access roads for the most part, and no amenities. There is a trail into Gleann Ceallach, but nothing more. One couldn't drive a lorry or a jeep very far into it. You need horses and tundra camels to move in and around, or your own two feet. Imagine then, Sikunder that you are a family; parents and four children say, and you decided to plot four hectares in Gleann Ceallach – the most the UN will let you claim in undeveloped territory." She sipped her coffee and continued. "You take your UN settlers credits and buy a tent, bedding, equipment to begin farming; buy or lease some horses or tundra camels depending on what little you have left; then you cross the Ceallach and penetrate the wilderness." She focused her deep eyes on me.

"Ten kilometres through trackless bush, following the Ceallach; it could take you a full day, and if you were lucky, you might find some likely land. You must set up your tent and camp, corral your beasts, preserve your food stores, and prepare the necessities. Then, you must stake out your plot, measuring as accurately as you can. Take too much or too little, and you will lose it when the UN surveyors eventually enter. This means cutting through the bush, over bog and brush. It could take days. Then you must begin to clear your land. If you wish to farm or ranch, the trees must be removed, and cutting down a 20 meter tall Pavonis pine is no mean feat, Sikunder. It could take you a day to do that and you may have scores or hundreds on your plot. Stumps must be blown up, brush hacked down and the wood removed. It is back breaking work when at best you may have a chainsaw and a small generator, and horses and tundra camels if you are lucky. And during all that," she added as her eyes continued to focus on me, "you have the weather to contend with. You have food and supplies that you must constantly go back and forth to get, always wary of those who have given up and decided it is easier to survive off the efforts and possessions of others. That, jawan, is what Gleann Ceallach is like."

"Are there no settlements? No protection in numbers?" I asked. It was difficult to imagine such hardship and struggle.

"Oh yes," Sittina said with a nod as she gestured for a passing *wallah* with a tall silver coffeepot to refill her cup, "there are several. Most are made up of a score or two of people, with two settlements containing up to a few hundred people, but most people live in groups of two or three families. That is how they defend themselves and survive. The *Chúsheng*, who are mostly nomadic, look for weaknesses and then set upon them. Sometimes it's merely for food; sometimes they are even hired to clear families off their plots so that other families can claim them. It can be somewhat barbaric," she finished.

"And the Gliesiuns?" I asked. I was curious how they had come into this.

"Ahh, the Gliesiuns. Normally, they cannot be bothered to come so far north, preferring instead their nomadic existence in the campusi to the south. Some have come north, however, hired by Klondike Corp to build the great eastern road up the Seleucus Vallis to Gleann Fearadadh. They tend to winter in the undeveloped valles like Gleann Ceallach or Gehon Vallis to the east. They are an unknown commodity here, though. They are dangerous when provoked so they tend to be left on their own. The ones you will see are mostly *Ossayuln* tribe but there are also *Tasyage* and *Ech'cha* in here as well. You will see them soon enough for MacShaka wants to begin patrols in the next few days to show the flag. He believes the UN will come here in the spring to survey and formally open the gleann." She allowed a slow smile to spread revealing her large white teeth. "We shall see what the Cardinal thinks of that."

"The Cardinal?" I asked. Sittina blinked at me in confusion before smiling. "Is it possible, in all that I have told you that I have forgotten to mention the Cardinal?"

"You have."

"Well, Sikunder, of all of the curiosities in Gleann Ceallach, the Cardinal is the most interesting. She runs a convent about 20 kilometres from here – a retreat for her nuns of Saint Brigid and those who take vows to defend her. I have never met her, but she is a most curious creature."

"She's a cardinal? Here on Samsāra?" I asked. As much as my religious upbringing was patchy at best, this seemed wrong.

"Maybe self-proclaimed, Sikunder, maybe not; I have asked to take the first patrol out as it is my hope to meet her as soon as possible."

I can't say I was that keen to meet her or any of the inhabitants of that gleann, but as fate would have it, I would meet the cardinal much sooner than I had hoped.

In the evening, as the deep darkness settled over us and the temperature dropped, I lay in my sleeping bag, hands behind my head as the remainder of the contubernium slept around me. Only a week before, I had been living the highlife in the open air down south, moving a herd of cows north over the Serberor Campus. It had been my own command and my own mission, and I had succeeded in my task against odds that no one had predicted. It had been a moment of real glory as my *wallahs* and I had brought those cows into Ophir, and now, as that glory faded, I faced the misery of my existence in a contubernium that saw me more as a joke and a bother. Living in a castrum surrounded by enemies on all sides, I saw, for a moment, the allure of desertion.

* * * * *

For two blessed weeks I had been beholden to no one. Whether it was tramping over the campus, mooching around Ophir and its saloons waiting for a barge, or vomiting over its side as we sailed to Agarum – I was my own man with five loyal underlings beneath me to service my needs.

For a brief time, I exercised the power of a despot.

As much as there may be a few inaccuracies in that statement, the spirit and intent of it is true. I rose when I pleased, lazed about while meals were prepared for me, parcelled out tasks on whomever I wished (save for Jindan, I doubt she would have brooked that kind of nonsense from me) and generally ran roughshod over my underlings with little thought for their feelings. Not that I was cruel or heartless, but I was their leader, their *Huzūra*, and I held the authority and the responsibility of completing our mission. It meant the power of pit and gallows, and the omnipotence of a duke of old. All that came to an end the moment I walked through the gate of Sommerkveld Castrum and I had no better illustration of that fact as when I was roused at 4 a.m. the following morning.

It was the kick that shocked me – a blow on my leg that wrenched me from my warm somnolence and a somewhat uncomfortable dream about playing poker with Jindan and knowingly, as I sat clad only in a pair of underwear, discarding a pair aces in order to draw a two and a five. I'm not sure what the loss of the hand might have meant, but the feeling, as I shook off my sleep, was subtly sexual in nature.

"Get up, jawan," a voice hissed. I heard a few more kicks, some muted curses from the cots around me before the voice growled, "Be in stables in 20 minutes."

Reality and an uncomfortable one; as I slipped out of my sleeping bag and into the cool air of the tent wearing only long underwear, I quickly remembered my place within the Legion and it was not one of exalted authority.

I was to clean the latrines.

Jindan bumped into me. She too was wearing only long underwear and it only accentuated the boyishness of her figure. She flashed a smile in the semi-darkness while donning her *salwars* and *kurta* shirt. I did the same, grunting as I eventually pulled on my boots while Usman yawned loud enough to wake Lukianos, who threw a boot at the boy. Amina Barre, our tiny Somalian, rubbed her eyes and then put on a heavy wool sweater and a sheepskin *postin* vest with the fur on the inside.

"I will make the coffee," she whispered as she exited the tent. The three of us followed minutes later, emerging into the pre-dawn darkness with vapourous breath in the near freezing temperatures.

"*Waa*! Why must winter come again so soon?" Usman whined as he clapped his hands against the chill and then rubbed his arms.

The four of us were soon drinking strong coffee in the mess tent, with Amina arranging a plate of *naan* bread as well. Jindan told her to leave off, a *wallah* would come along soon enough, but Amina would not be dissuaded.

"It was what I did for my family before I came here," she said in reply. "I miss it."

"Go back home then, *tshergóttey*," Usman said through a mouthful of bread. Jindan slapped him in the back of the head sending masticated bread over the table. "*Ahk*! Why did you do that?" he whined.

"*Adhajal gagri chhalakat jaaye*," she groused into her mug. She looked at Amina and said, "A half-filled pot splashes more."

"*Wax*," Usman rubbed the back of his head and glared daggers at Jindan. I noted with an inward grin that he wouldn't dare lift a hand against her.

"The latrines," she added. "We should split up. It will take an hour to scrub each alone, but we will be done in time for breakfast."

"Then we are tasked to move firewood," Usman said while deep in a case of the sulks. "After that, back to building the walls." He looked upon Jindan with a face soured by embarrassment and anger. "You did not have to do that these past weeks."

"No, *gadahā*," she said, "we were sleeping out in tents in the campus and being chased by Black Hand *guṭṭa* while you lazed in your sleeping bag and ate such grand meals." She looked at me and winked, which seemed to infuriate Usman even more. "Is that not right, *Sirdar*?"

No way was I going to be dragged into that mess, so I shrugged, finished my coffee, and decided I'd hide away from the conflict by scrubbing toilets.

As much as I delight to entertain with my stories of terrifying events where I am dragged, often against my will, into situations where only a near death experience will satiate the reader, I must come out with all honesty and state that those minor episodes are the exception to the rule. Sadly, the norm was far less pleasant than charging up a beach to attack a Tong fort, or facing down a Black Hand bully and vomiting out a mess of cank fish and merlot while Lukianos screamed "Cholera" in a horrified stage whisper and winked at me. No, the true norm of my years in the Legion had me not armed with a Khyber knife or a pulse rifle but with a toilet brush. And so, after my hiatus of freedom, it was with a colossal pout that I sat alone in the foetid solitude of my existence scrubbing feces and swabbing urine until the room reeked of bleach and I figured it would pass the muster of even Havildar Cong, who was the most particular of inspectors prior to his morning constitutional.

After storing away the cleaning supplies, I exited to come upon the dawn, or what I assumed was dawn as the obfuscated light seeped through the oppressive low cloud of the valley. The rain had stopped, which was a small comfort, though the temperature was still hovering just a few degrees above zero. I ducked back into our tent, now empty as the rest of the contubernium sat down for breakfast, to retrieve my wool sweater.

I had no more entered when I found myself trapped, for there stood Jindan, half dressed as she shed a pair of filthy, noisome *salwars* and dropped them into a laundry bag.

"Sikunder," she said as she reached into her barrack box for a faded pair of clean *salwars*. She sat on her cot and pulled them on. "I had a wee accident," she said as she pointed to the laundry bag. "The composting toilet burst." She was smiling, though just barely. The smell was awful.

"*Jaan hai to Jahan Hai,* my people say," she added as she stood up.

"Which is?" I asked as I took a step back. The look in her eye gave me pause. I'd rather have faced a bear.

"If there's life, Sikunder, then there's the world."

I took a step closer to the door. "Which means?"

She smiled that pretty smile that was as alluring as it was frightening. "Things matter, but only because you are alive."

"Well," I said trying to buy time.

"Are you frightened of me, Sikunder?" she asked as she took another step forward and grabbed my hand; it seemed huge in her dainty paw. She had me and she knew it. Though her grip was light, I could no more wrench my hand away than I could pull out my own heart.

"Uh, no," I replied with a choke.

"I think you are," she said with a wink as she stepped a bit closer. "A great *bahadur* such as you; a *barra* jawan who charged ashore with MacShaka and MacGrogan-Singh with the pipes playing and the Tongs shooting at you in the Coloe Vallis. You, such a *pukka* young man, afraid of a *chota* wee girl like me. I wonder why?"

"I'm not afraid," I said with all of the credibility of a philandering evangelist.

"I think you are, Sikunder," She replied. "I think that is good. You should be afraid of me." With that, she stood on her tip toes and gave me the sweetest little peck on my nose before walking past me and exiting the tent.

I sank to my cot as if I had just finished a battle. Suddenly, a few more weeks back in the campus without Jindan looked very enticing.

* * * * *

"Sikunder!" Lukianos called out when I paused for a moment to warm my hands over a fire, "get your ass back over here and fill up these sandbags!"

I had hoped to warm myself for just a few moments, but it was not to be. For the last four hours, ever since a hasty meal of rice and cold pork for breakfast, Usman, Amina, Jindan, and myself had been hard at it carrying out the backbreaking work of filling sandbags and piling them near the gabions where another group of jawans had the unenviable task of dropping them into said gabions. As we filled the bags, Lukianos and Yee Hong-miao unloaded sand from the back of a rotten six-wheeled Mitsubishi lorry while Fung Wai-ting and Makemba Adoula did the same from another lorry. Muneer Al-Shahid-Mahmood was with a half dozen other jawans a kilometre away digging out the glacial fill from a cliff face. It was all hands on deck with another contubernium working on the opposite wall while across the Ceallach a third contubernium was pulling down a few trees, and a fourth was packing down glacial fill on the maidan in order to fill in a bog that continued to soak through. It was all miserable work, and the damp penetrating cold only made it worse.

"Come now," Lukianos griped as he shovelled sand and gravel off of the back of the lorry. "It is only an hour until lunch. Have your rest then, Sikunder. If you need motivation, remember that even now, the *Chúsheng* may be watching and hoping to hit you over our incomplete walls."

Well, that was one way to motivate me. A few thoughts about the idea of being in some sniper's rifle site were enough for me to dig in and find my energy reserves. Soaked from sweat and with my *salwars* and *kurta* thick with clay and sand, I picked up the pace as much as possible carrying each 20 kilogram sandbag to the jawans near the gabions before jogging back for the next one. I was puffing like a bellows as Usman and Amani filled and tied off the bags. Jindan was my carrying and filling partner – we swapped out with Usman and Amani every 30 minutes or so – and she was puffing as hard as I; likely more, as her elfin frame hauled bags nearing half of her weight.

This was the type of brute hard labour made famous in the Legion, for we were bereft of the kind of heavy equipment in the colony that any other military force would have had to make this task easier. It was partly due to cost, for KlondikeCorp – the faceless multinational corporation that equipped and maintained the Legion – did what it could to maintain its bottom line. It was also partly because of the difficulty of getting heavy equipment deep into the vallis. So, while most other military forces would have had the walls done in a few days using front end loaders and dump trucks, we would spend 10 hours a day with shovels and sore backs to accomplish the same task in a few weeks.

"Sikunder," Jindan panted as she paused by the growing pile of sandbags at the base of the lorry, "to think that we missed many days of this because the cattle were stolen from us by the Black Hand." She brushed a muddy strand of hair from her eyes and flashed an exhausted smile. "I wish now that we had not been so quick to recover the cows. I wish that we had chased the Black Hand *kutte ke tatte* further south for a few days."

"Aye," I replied breathless, "and what would they have done without us?"

"Not much fucking more than we are with you!" Lukianos roared. "Get on with it already!"

My arms were like rubber and my legs wobbled as I continued the misery of moving the sandbags to the gabions. I was approaching my limit, and Jindan was clearly at hers as she stumbled and staggered, when Usman called out that our 30 minutes was up.

"*I bow to Lord Vishnu,*" Jindan chanted with little breath, "*the one master of the Universe.*" Her eyes were closed as she bent over and stretched her weary back. "*Who is ever peaceful, who reclines on the great serpent bed, from whose navel springs the lotus of creative power.*" She paused to wipe the sweat from her forehead, leaving a thick smear of reddish clay. "*Who is the supreme being, who supports the entire universe, who is all pervading as the sky, who is dark like the clouds,*" she looked at me and allowed a exhausted smile. "*Who has a beautiful form; the Lord Lakshmi, the lotus-eyed one, whom the yogis are able to perceive through meditation. He who is the destroyer of the fear of Samsāra.*"

"Feel better?" I gasped as I took a shovel from Usman.

"Yes," she replied as she took an empty bag from Amani. She knelt down before me and opened the bag. Looking me in the eyes, she said in a most suggestive tone, "I am ready for you to fill me, *Sirdar.*"

"Oh," I said as I blushed. I averted my eyes and focused on the task at hand. Oh, how I focused on shovelling sand at that moment!

At first, I thought Sittina had taken some pity on me. After a hasty meal in the mess tent, she pulled me aside as I was about to snatch a few minutes rest for my weary body, and informed me that I was to accompany Lukianos out to the dig site where we were getting our sand and gravel. I was thrilled with the idea of escaping Jindan for a few hours, and I jumped at it. When I arrived at the banks of sand and gravel a kilometre away from the castrum, however, my enthusiasm vanished like the ethics of a two-term Member of Parliament. For standing hands on hips and smiling as she spotted my cringing form in the back of the lorry was Jemadar Er-hong Kim, second-in-command of our decuria and a Manchu Messalina of capricious cruelty.

She wasn't alone of course, for beside her stood four of the decuria's biggest brutes – *badmashes* to a man, they hovered around her in their filth while holding spades and eyeing me with grinning facades that reminded of me of cats looking upon a mouse. Lukianos backed the lorry to the bank and Er-hong Kim stepped into the box.

"We' now, jawan decide to come and wo'k fo' a living instead of p'aying cowboy." I was waiting for the blow that usually accompanied any dialogue she and I shared, for she had gone to great pains to ensure that I was fully aware of the contempt she held for me – I had joined the Legion for adventure, and she, for survival.

None came, however.

I shifted focus to the four towering roughnecks standing on the bank behind her – all filthy Easter Island statues looking upon me with that familiar mixture of amusement and disdain. Would the abuse come from them? It had before. The two Uzbeks –

Hamid Salih and Babur Arlov had tortured me for an hour during my first week in the decuria, beating me with a switch while they taught me the Uzbek lullaby, *O'zbekona alla*. The Sikh, a burly bargee by the name of Aneel Brara-Singh, delighted in kicking me awake if ever he had the opportunity to shake me for a watch. The fourth, a bad-tempered alcoholic Russian, painted with tattoos all over his gladiator's frame, was named Yaropolk Kupchenko; he had once simply blackened my eye while deep in his cups. These four brutes I normally steered very clear of, and to have them and Kim in the same spot spelled trouble for me.

I could have choked Sittina.

Kupchenko tossed me a shovel. "Start shovelling, *pizda*," he said in a slur. He was already half cut.

I dug in while every fibre of me waited for the blows.

They didn't come.

After a few minutes of silent shovelling, I allowed a cautious look at my bruiser comrades, but they were focused on the task at hand while Kim smoked and looked at me slantindicular and with a frightening and tiny grin on her face. Was she planning something bigger than just a mere beating? She hated me, I remember thinking, and here was Gaia surrounded by four of her Titans; I was a mere nod away from spitting teeth.

Yet nothing happened.

Lukianos drove off to be replaced by another lorry, and again we filled it with little chatter and much gruelling work. I couldn't figure it as the first hour passed – not a single action of abuse. I mused on it over a coffee as we rested for a few breathless minutes between lorries. Weeks before, she had gleefully shoved me aboard a riverboat to ride shotgun with the hope that I would never return and now, she was, almost pleasant? Was it possible that some profound change had come over her in the last two weeks? Could that absolute hatred of hers – the kind that put her mythical Greek equivalent, Erida, to shame – have been overcome? If so, how? What singular event could have created such a colossal shift in our relationship?

Bogged down by fear and paranoia, the obvious escaped me, at least for a while. Eventually I cottoned onto the reason.

It was Jindan.

Jindan was a favourite of MacShaka ever since he had bought her from slavery three years before. By extension, she was a favourite of the decuria as a *wallah*, and now that she was a jawan, that favour grew. Her obvious feelings for me changed my status – from mere punching bag to grudging comrade. I didn't know what to make of it, but one thing was sure, I certainly appreciated it.

We returned at supper and I was so bone weary I nearly skipped the meal to find some sleep. I couldn't, however, as we had the watch at 20:00 until midnight. So after a hasty supper and an hour of deep sleep, the decuria was back up in the towers watching the darkness. I was lucky to have Usman with me as it meant we could sneak naps and not be caught. Fortunately, all was quiet, and my first day back in the cantonment ended 20 hours after it began.

* * * * *

This was our existence for a week – rise early to clean latrines or stables, a hasty breakfast, then 10 or more solid hours of arduous labour to build up the cantonment's defences. We were fortunate to get more help in the form of the 20 constables who would be moving into the cantonment when it was finished, along with a score or so of hired workers from Agarum. All told, we made short work of the walls, building up three layers of one meter gabions that were four rows thick. It made for a solid wall that could not be broken by any weapon save for those held by the Legion, and everyone felt much safer in that lonely wasteland.

That feeling of comfort was buoyed by the fact that we'd had no issues with the *Chúsheng* for nearly a week. No sniping, no sightings, nothing at all to suggest they were around. Even the traders moving across the Ceallach said they had little contact, so we figured that our imposing castrum rising from the bog had terrified them into rancorous obedience.

That is, until they fired upon us one morning.

Eight days after my return, while our contubernium was laying out razor wire along the top of the wall, the *Chúsheng* made their presence known with a single shot from the forest opposite us. The bullet snipped through the razor wire near Usman who shrieked, dropped his end of the coil, and raced for the nearest tower like a stung terrier. I'd like to say I did the same, that my sense of self-preservation kicked in and that I had reacted with a fight or flight response with an emphasis on flight.

It didn't.

Instead, I opted for standing moon-eyed in the open while a second round ricocheted off a razor wire stake a meter away from me.

"Sikunder!" Sittina shouted from the nearest tower, "don't just stand there! Get your ass over here!"

A third round fanned by my face; still, I was frozen to the spot.

"Sikunder! Move!"

My legs finally thawed, my brain finally engaged, and fight or flight was in full response as I sprinted towards the nearest tower. A fourth round hit the tower gabions as I leapt over them and into cover.

"What kind of a fucking idiot are you?" Sittina asked as she cuffed my head.

Yee Hong-miao and Makemba Adoula were returning shots at the trees, but little came of it. No other shots were fired and only a pair of faint thermal images could be seen fading into the dense brush.

MacShaka appeared amongst us, naked save for his boots and *salwars*. He held a pulse rifle in his hands and his deep dark eyes had an evil glint. Othello had nothing on him.

"It appears we hae tae clean out that damned brush again tomorrow."

Part Four
Ambuscade

The following morning, as the first real dusting of autumn snow fell, our contubernium dragged out our mephitic winter clothing from storage, including thicker woollen long johns, sheepskin *postin* vests, and heavy gloves. After a brief breakfast and coffee, we were assigned the daily task of clearing trees on the far side of Gleann Ceallach, some 300 or so meters from the walls of the castrum. At any other time we would have been thrilled with the thought of escaping the gruelling work of filling and moving sandbags or the equally punishing task of packing down gravel in the *maidan*, but now that the *Chúsheng* were lurking out there again, our enthusiasm waned. While two other contuberniums continued the labourious process of unloading sandbags from lorries and filling the mesh gabions around the central tower in the castrum, and the fourth continued the arduous task of packing down a new layer of gravel over the bog that our *maidan* had once again become, we slogged through a few centimetres of new fallen snow to the far tree line armed with rifles, chainsaws, and axes. With a line of draft horses following for the heavy work of moving the brush and branches back to the castrum for use as a defensive abatis before the walls, we arrived beneath the towering gloom and thick brush of the forest. Sittina had us gather around.

"Alright, we have a day of this, so don't get all miserable about it too early." She looked at us all for a moment and said, "Lukianos, take Sikunder and Barre to do a sweep to the north. Go out a few hundred meters and take a look around. Any issues call it in. Got it?"

Lukianos nodded solemnly and then glanced at Amina and myself. "Come, let us go."

While the remainder of the contubernium unloaded equipment and set to work thinning the trees and reducing cover, Lukianos led us into the deepening murk of the monumental forest, pushing through ferns and brush and scrambling over the moss covered boulders, rotting branches, and slippery tree roots. At some point, many thousands of years before, this valley had been filled with a glacier, for the mossy rock piles and larger rounded erratics, some as considerable as a bus, were clear evidence of that destructive, distant past. Now, within the deep verdant gloom, these same rocks and boulders provided near perfect cover for anyone wanting to watch us, let alone shoot at us.

We scrambled over the terrain, picking our way carefully and as quietly as possible. There was no snow beneath the soaring canopy, but the footing was treacherous and the hillsides, as we approached them, grew steep and dangerous. After about 20 minutes, with the distant buzz of chainsaws shattering the soundless shadow beginning to fade, Lukianos bade us pause. As we sipped water from canteens and puffed like bellows, he pulled out a compu-pad and examined the topographical map and our GPS position.

"There is a point to the northeast," he said as he gestured through the forest and up the hill, "that may afford us an opportunity to look upon anyone coming south. It is a stream and the gulley it is in appears to have fewer trees." He glanced at me and tiny Amina who looked ridiculous in her oversized *postin* and massive pulse rifle. "Can you keep up, little rabbit?" he asked with a fatherly smile. Amina nodded and smiled back.

"I will not fall behind."

"Good. Alright, Sikunder, you may lead the way."

I paused, terrified at the thought.

"Bah," Lukianos snarled, "He who becomes a sheep is eaten by the wolf." He gave me a push and I stumbled forward.

I had my pulse rifle at the ready as I led us northeast and up the rocky side of the gleann. It took us nearly 15 minutes to flounder our way through a trackless forest that thickened with ferns and bracken over the piled rocks slick with moss, before the sound of rushing water intruded and the vegetation on the forest floor opened into a narrow gulley of fern and moss. We were still beneath the canopy but our new vantage point afforded us an unrestricted view of the stream on flatter ground below. Lukianos motioned us to take a position behind a boulder and pointed at the stream. "You see the log, Sikunder?" he asked as he smoothed his long white beard, "The one that someone has put across the stream for a bridge?"

I did, and it meant no good for us. There was no reason to ford the stream this deep within the forest save to allow movement south down the gleann under cover; movement of the *Chúsheng* no doubt.

"Amina," Lukianos said as he settled himself down with a pair of binoculars. "Make us some tea please."

Amina set up the tiny camp stove, poured water into a pot and began the process of boiling tea. I nibbled on some hard bread as I looked upon the bridge below and listened to the distant work on the castrum. It was a very dull, remote, sound now – a mild intrusive drone of civilization – and nearly overwhelmed by the tumbling glacial waters of the stream. For a few moments, as I sipped scalding tea and peered into the gloom, I was painfully aware of my miniscule place on this alien world. The trees with their imperial beryl canopy far above us, the bracken, the ferns and moss – so like Earth and yet, so distinctly alien. The fiddleheads, some as tall as a man, with red dots on their leaves; the bracken that grew my height, thick with tiny deep blue berries that were surprisingly sweet with an aftertaste of mint; the creepers of trailing lichen; and the scores of moss varietals that carpeted everything. So familiar, yet with an exoticness that could not be ignored.

It was moments like these that made my time on Samsāra a true wonder.

We sat huddled in the damp cold for an hour or so, enjoying our tea and a cheerless meal of *naan* bread and *londi*, a spiced goat jerky that soon followed it. Amina napped with her arms pulled into her *postin* vest while Lukianos and I kept a solemn watch, modestly happy in our discomfort and potential danger as we were away from the heavy work of tree clearing.

"Truly, Sikunder," Lukianos said as he popped a morsel of *londi* into his mouth, "this will not be a posting that is a joy. This will be like going to Bonitatus far to the north, or worse, Caloris or Zayra. You do not know true misery until you have been posted there."

"Were you ever there?" I asked. I'd heard of those places, camps isolated deep in the northern wilderness of the Cylenne Vallis along the trail to the Tiberian Porto and the gold camps beyond in Eros. It was some 400 kilometres north in a region of Samsāra far harsher that this.

"Once, for a brief period," he said as he sipped his tea. "I was in another decuria then, a few years before your time here, the 4th Decuria of the Accipiter Centuria; my first posting. I and four other new jawans were flown in; otherwise it would have taken us weeks to travel by boat and tundra camel. Eros did not exist then, but the camp of Zayra did, and the UN, feeling that settlers would make their way north on their own in larger numbers, set up a decuria there. It was a hellish place, nothing but mud, ice, and snow; a few hundred people clinging to life in an existence that could only be described as abominable. People arrived every week, and nearly as many died from the cold, from hunger, from disease, and from their own hand. After our arrival, I found that we had been brought in to replace two jawans who had hung themselves, another who had deserted and disappeared, and two more who had been murdered by a fellow jawan in a drunken brawl; and our decuria still only had 30 jawans instead of its usual 50 or so. Each month I was there, and I was fortunate to only be there for four months in total before I caught a terrible lung infection and had to be flown out to Ophir, we lost more jawans to death and desertion. When I finally did leave, we had 22 out of our 50. The numbers, even now, Sikunder, don't change much; a posting to Zayra or Caloris is nearly a death sentence. The bad of the morning," he paused to look around the forest, "becomes worse by the night. Mark my words; there will be much blood here now that the Legion has arrived."

Lukianos wasn't making me feel good, not that I was feeling good about the situation anyway. Each hour seemed to solidify my anxiety that this new posting was indeed going to be horribly dangerous, and after another hour of shivering in the cold watching for activity, the sudden distant movement in the gloom only confirmed it.

"We have company," Lukianos muttered as he shook Amina.

Lurking among the shadows below were a handful of flitting figures, perhaps seven or so, trailing pulse rifles and certainly looking like they were up to no good. Lukianos called it in to the castrum while Amina and I found a position where we could cover the figures with our pulse rifles.

"About 100 meters away," Lukianos breathed. He was an old hand, having been in the Legion these past five years. He took a bead on the lead figure who now stood at the foot of the bridge. "It is better to tie your donkey than to go searching for it afterwards, Sikunder." A moment later he squeezed the trigger and his pulse rifle jumped. The lead figure dropped while the others froze for a moment before scattering like deer into the murk.

"Are you crazy?" I hissed as he fired a second shot. "What are you doing?"

A fusillade of shots returned, sending bullets fanning around us. We were well protected, but the last thing I had been mentally preparing myself for this morning as I had been downing my coffee and toast was a firefight with a handful of murderers because Lukianos had taken it upon himself to pick a fight.

"Now you've eaten the bull, will you leave the tail?" he asked me with a cackle. The old Adonis was full of wit. "They are clearly here for trouble," Lukianos added as he peered into his scope and fired. "Ahh, *filos*," he said with a smile at the figure who fell back into the bracken clutching his ear, "you should not stick your head up." He guffawed while I wriggled away from the cover of our boulder to a smaller one a few meters away. Once there, I rested my pulse rifle on its mossy top, and took aim at a figure nearly hidden by a tree. "Come now, Sikunder," Lukianos called out as he fired a pair of shots. "It is better to be the head of a fox than the tail of a lion!"

"Jesus, shut up," I muttered as I fired a shot. Bark flew from the tree, and what little of the figure I could see disappeared; so much for my shooting skills. Another figure was crouching behind a rock, and I let fly a few shots at him, but again, my often ineffectual aiming meant that the fellow was merely driven into cover. Not that I minded really. I'd only knowingly killed one person during my six months on Samsāra – that old Chinese Black Hand soldier forced to fight us or die. I'd killed him in hand-to-hand combat in a trench in the Coloe Vallis five months before, and I still saw his face in my mind's eye as I shot him at close range while he lay in the mud at my feet. No, if I could avoid it, I wanted as little blood on my hands as possible. Winging them though, I figured, was fair, so I aimed for an outstretched foot I spied behind a log. I held my breath and gently squeezed the trigger. The pulse rifle bucked and I saw the foot jerk as the bullet punched through it. The howl of agony was voluble over the roaring of the stream.

"Much better, Sikunder," Lukianos chuckled. More bullets flew about us, plucking at branches and ricocheting off of rocks. Amina was huddled at the edge of the boulder, peering out every so often to loose off a shot. I doubt she was any more effective than I was, but she was a willing participant at least until a bullet nicked her jaw.

"Sikunder!" Lukianos shouted as Amina fell back, her eyes wide in horror as she held her hand to her bloody jaw. I crawled to her as she lay back on the moss, terrified and in agony as blood sopped her glove.

"Keep the pressure on," I said as I pulled a first aid kit from my pack. I tore open a bio-dressing, pulled her hand away from the torn skin on her jaw, and then placed it on the mess of the wound. "It's alright," I said as soothingly as I could, though I was horrified by the blood and flailed flesh. She was paling and going into shock as I rolled into a recovery position, and then I picked up my rifle to take her position at the edge of the boulder.

"Fuck sakes, Lukianos, are they running away yet?" We'd picked a fight, for propriety's sake really and with an expectation that the *Chúsheng*, or whoever these fellows were, would flee at the first shot. They had not and they showed every indication that they were there for the long haul.

"It appears they think they can force a crossing," Lukianos confessed as he fired a pair of shots to drop another figure who was trying to run across the log bridge. "They feel quite confident it appears."

"No kidding," I replied as I inserted a new magazine into my pulse rifle. I felt for another power pack, ensuring I still had it in my webbing. I was down to 50 percent already. "Is the contubernium coming or what?"

"They are coming, Sikunder," Lukianos declared with a calm composure so much at odds with my jittery, screaming panic. "Time has turns, and the year has weeks."

"Oh my God will you stop!" I retorted after I fired a shot into a tree. "Maybe we should have got them to come up before we started shooting."

"Then the *Chúsheng* would have been across, Sikunder," he rejoined with patient tones, like a teacher instructing a dull child. "Where would we be then?"

"Maybe less dead than what we will be if the others don't come soon." As I said this, a bullet nicked the boulder beside my face, spraying with me with shards of rock that opened my cheek, brow, and nose. I fell back, blinking away the dust and grit from my eyes and squawking in pain as blood dribbled down my face to soak my collar and scarf. I brushed it aside, smearing the gore all over my face, and picked up my rifle.

"Sikunder," Lukianos called out, his voice suddenly dripping concern. "There are people opposite us and further up the stream. They are trying to flank us. You must cover them!"

I moved quickly to the other end of the boulder, pausing for a moment to check on Amina. She had fainted away and was now unconscious; I wondered for moment if her jaw was broken. As I squatted and took stock of the changing situation, it was beginning to appear much more desperate. The stream ran down through a narrow gulch, steep, rocky and thick with brush on either side. It was difficult if not impossible to cross save for on a log. One log had been placed purposely below, but now I wondered, since Lukianos had seen figures climbing the hill, if there might be another log crossing further up. I glanced around the boulder, saw elusive movement in the thick brush, and fired a pair of shots. I certainly had no expectations of hitting anything, but I wanted them to know that they had been seen. More movement, flitting from tree to tree and more shots; it kept them off guard I hoped, but I had to admit as the minutes passed, that their determination was very worrying. With two hit and likely dead, and others injured, their resolve to force a crossing demonstrated a confidence that belied their characterization as a loose, poorly armed gang of thugs uninterested in a stand up fight. It was unnerving and I said as much to Lukianos between shots.

"Yes," he replied. His face was grave as he inserted a new power pack into his rifle. "It is surprising. They must have more numbers than I thought."

"That's great," I groused as I brushed more blood off my face. The pain was growing and I glanced at my watch. If we'd been shooting for five minutes, I'd be surprised, yet it felt like an hour. We were pinned down, yet also unwilling to give up our position and let the *Chúsheng* cross the stream. However, with Amina injured, we'd be slowed down carrying her. The best course was to sit tight, conserve our ammo, and pick them off until the remainder of the contubernium arrived; which was hopefully soon.

I saw movement on a rocky outcrop some 30 meters up the stream. A head popped up and then disappeared. They were in a good position there; I needed to keep them down. I peered through my scope, saw the head appear again, and I fired a quick shot. I missed, but the head disappeared and I was willing to bet they'd think twice about popping up again. The din of the shootout was deafening as bullets fanned around us, punching into bark, snapping off rock, but suddenly the intensity faded. Lukianos must have noticed it too, for he crowed, "I think they are putting some thought into their attack. Maybe they realize it is not such a good idea. Aided by Athena and move your hand!"

It was true, the sound of gunfire had faded to nothing and neither of us saw any movement. It was as if they'd given up, but I wasn't about to let my guard down. They had a strong position above us and I was keeping a keen eye up there. There was nothing, however; all activity had ended.

"For the enemy that leaves, build a golden bridge. I think they have given up," Lukianos said as he knelt by Amina. "Yes, her jaw is fractured, I think," he said after lifting the dressing. She was awake now, staring into the trees, and terrified. While Lukianos looked on, I moved to squat beside her and hold her hand.

"You're alright," I said trying to sooth her fears as tears filled her eyes. I must have looked terrible as I held her hand and waited for the others to arrive. Dripping gore down my tartan scarf and onto my *postin* and *chapan*, I gave up trying to brush it aside and let it run. The silence was imposing, now that the gunfire had ended and the sound of chainsaws was gone. As Lukianos scanned the log below and the rocky outcropping above looking for movement and I held Amina's hand and prayed for help to arrive, I suddenly heard voices and scrambling over rocks. In moments, Muneer pushed his way through the brush to appear. He moved aside and squatted when I pointed to the outcrop above us. His pulse rifle came up and he looked for a reason to fire. Sittina was next, followed by Usman, our Chinese twins, Jindan who gave a cry at the sight of my bloodied face, and finally Makemba, who was also our medic.

"That is a familiar injury," she said as she knelt beside Amina. She tapped the livid scare on her own jaw where she'd been shot six months before as we had battled Sindhi pirates on a paddlewheeler. "You will be fine."

"What the fuck did you start here?" Sittina seethed as she corralled Lukianos and I. "No one said to shoot up the fucking place!" She was furious, ready to strike. She pulled a bio-dressing from her webbing and tossed it to me. "Clean up your face, Sikunder, you look a fucking mess." She focused her attention on Lukianos who sat there looking grim. "MacShaka is not going to be pleased with you two; not at all."

* * * * *

"Just what the fuck dae ye think ye're daen, openin' up on every movin' target in the gleann? Who the fuck gave permission fer that?"

MacShaka was in a rare tear, focusing most of his ire on Lukianos who sat on a bench in the operations tent looking at him with bold vexation in his eyes while I held a bandage to my torn face.

"Well?" he thundered as he took a chair and sat down opposite of the mercurial Greek. "I'm fuckin' waitin'."

"Bah," Lukianos returned with a growl. "Everything about the wedding is difficult and the bride is pregnant! They were armed *Chúsheng* and crossing a bridge created deep in the brush that was well hidden. Their actions were suspect. I did not want them to come upon the rest of the contubernium unawares."

"Ham-a-haddie!" MacShaka snorted in derision. "How the fuck would that hae happened since ye called it in?" MacShaka was working his way up to a new fury. "Hoots mon, ye're a bletherin' fuckin' skite! Ye picked a fight when one may not hae needed pickin'!"

I sat watching the exchange, frankly surprised. They were obviously *Chúsheng*, and for the last three weeks, these people had been harassing us, shooting and making a general bother. Lukianos had taken it upon himself to stop another attack and had knocked off a couple for their pains. The fact that poor Amina was in the medical tent with a fractured jaw and I was sitting there dripping gore on my boots was a small price to pay, I would have thought. Not so MacShaka.

"Fuck sakes, jawan," he groused. He glared at him balefully and then glanced at me. "You fucking two probably just started a war."

"Whoever gets burnt by hot soup blows the yogurt. I would have thought, *Huzūra*, that the *Chúsheng* firing upon us first was cause for retaliation. They are criminals," Lukianos mumbled as he massaged his temples. "The Black Hand did as much and we punished them in Cole Vallis. Why should the *Chúsheng* be any different?"

MacShaka sat back in his chair, which creaked alarmingly. Though it was cold inside the tent, he was dressed only in his *kurta* and scarlet *salwars*. "Hoch aye," he retorted, his voice thoughtful. "The Black Hand pushed their luck, there's no' a doubt. And we made them pay for it, we did; a one off though for the crabbit bastards. They learned no' tae push their luck sae far wi' the Legion. These people, Lukianos, these people are different. Nae organization, nae discipline, nae a man we can sit down wi' tae set them straight. We'll hae a sair pech in this land, we will, fightin' wi' these bastards every day and watchin' our jawans die off. It's made worse by the fact that the *Chúsheng* just may be close tae some of the Gliesiun tribes as weel."

"We have not heard that," Lukianos returned.

"No, I doubt ye would. I didnae hae it in mind tae sit down wi' ye, ye dour bampot, and explain ma thoughts tae ye." MacShaka glanced at his havildars: Sittina, Jagdeep Sanghera Singh, Cong Fu-chi, and Mohammad Khan. The four of them stood grave faced and solemn as judges as they considered his words. "Fact is, we dinnae ken what we've gotten intae yet and I wasnae prepared tae take the fight tae the *Chúsheng* or the Gliesiuns or whoever until we haed the layout o' the land. Your foolish fucking shenanigans o' the day just made that harder."

Silence intruded as MacShaka sat brooding. "Weel, there's no' a thing tae be done now. The Deputy Warden of the Constabulary here says he's taking a patrol out tomorrow now that we are watching the frontier. Since you two are sae fired up tae shoot up the place, ye can join him in the saddle an' freeze your arses in the dreich for the day; the sleet and snow might cool yer hotheaded tempers."

Lukianos said nothing, and although I was about to protest, I noted Sittina's glance, the slightest shake of her head, and wisely held my tongue.

"Away wi' ye," MacShaka snapped as he stood up. Sittina ushered us out of the operations tent.

"Lukianos, go get some supper. Sikunder," she said to me as flakes of snow began to fall. "Go see the doc and have him patch up that ugly face of yours."

* * * * *

"I am sorry, Sikunder," Lukianos grunted as he took a seat beside me in the mess tent. The choleric old Greek was looking far older now, his face grey and eyes weary. He sipped coffee as I struggled to eat rice against the layers of skin repair strips our drunken medico had splattered over my cuts. I knew I looked horrific, but Lukianos was polite enough to ignore my gruesome visage and focus on his coffee. "Tomorrow we will at least be out in the saddle, which is much better than skulking about the trees or filling sandbags. The constables are a curious lot, but they are friendly after a fashion. It will be a fine day and we will be the first jawans to see Gleann Ceallach. But I am sorry for your injuries."

"How was Amina?" I inquired. I knew that he had just returned from seeing her.

"The doctor has her well drugged," Lukianos replied with a sigh. "She will be fine. A mild fracture; the gash hurt the most. She will be back with the contubernium tomorrow filling sandbags and freezing." He sighed. "*I glóssa kókala den échei, allá kókala tsakízei,*" he muttered into his cup.

"Which is?"

"The tongue, Sikunder, has no bones, yet it crushes. It is a hard thing to hear that I may have started a war."

"You didn't know," I remonstrated.

"Still," he said but did not finish. Abruptly he stood and announced, "It would be best if we got some sleep, Sikunder." He allowed a small wintry smile. "It will be a very long day in the saddle, I believe."

With that he returned to our tent while I struggled with the remainder of my meal. The mess tent was emptying; most of the jawans had had a long day of it, and were eating with haste before either retiring to the relative warmth of their tents, or going on duty in the frosty towers to watch the Stygian darkness of the gleann. A handful of *wallahs* were cleaning up, stacking trays and dishes and taking them in for washing. Another was sweeping the matting while one of the youngest was making a fresh pot of coffee. When the last jawan left, I signalled the coffee *wallah* for a cup. She was Wandina Omaswa, a 10 year old hellcat who had spent two weeks with me herding cattle. She came across with a silver coffee pot and a small demitasse on a saucer.

"*Sahib*," she giggled with a charming smile. She poured the coffee and placed the pot on the table. "Are you in much pain?" she asked as she very gently touched my ear near the bandages.

"No, Wandina, not too much; not as sore as you and I were after a week in the saddle," I replied with a wink. "And to think, it was only two weeks ago that you were cutting the painter of that Black Hand boat in the night while we stole back our herd of cattle."

She would have blushed had she been able, my little Ugandan cutthroat. Instead she curtsied, such an odd thing to see with her dressed in child sized scarlet *salwars* with a *kurta* shirt hanging down to her knees. Almost a doll she was, and I reflected, as she took the pot away with her, that in six years she too would have her opportunity to fight and die for the Legion. I thought of poor Amina, as she lay in the medical tent. She was an unlikely candidate for the Legion, hardly the stuff of jawan legend (not that I was either) but her injuries had clearly distressed her beyond what they should have. Obviously no one liked being shot – I was shot two weeks after my arrival by a Black Hand banditto while attacking them with a tribe of Gliesiuns and I certainly didn't enjoy it as I lay in a freezing bog thinking I was about to die – but she seemed to be taking it especially hard. I hoped I would have an opportunity to sit down with her soon. Maybe hearing of my own first injury would help.

I was beginning to feel sorry for myself, injured as I was and being punished for following Lukianos' lead. Back in the castrum for only a week after nearly two weeks away with no more thought for me than a pariah dog. It was enough to give one the sulks, and I'll admit, as I sat there over my cup of coffee, I was feeling a pretty decent case of them coming on. In fact, I was near tears when the door opened and in strode MacShaka, all lordly and bestial – like some Yeti with a dukedom. He stood there looking at the coffee for a moment, while I tried to sink into my chair, before noticing me out of the corner of his eye.

"Callan," he said to Wandina with a smile and a wink, "gie us a wee cup o' coffee, lass, and bring it over tae the table wi' the greetin' faced keelie sittin' at it."

MacShaka came over, striding like Polyphemus in scarlet trousers and black skull cap, as he read a compu-pad. After pausing at the table to finish, he slipped it into the pocket of his open *sherwani* coat and took a chair opposite me. "Well, lad," he said as Wandina brought him his cup of coffee. He spared her another wink after she curtsied and smiled. Looking on me as she left, he said, "Ye've a face like a saft tattie, Sikunder. What could possibly be botherin' ye now, ye torn faced wifie?"

I sipped my coffee, unwilling to commit to a conversation that might get me nothing more than a slap on the back of the head or a poke in the chest. "Nothing, *Huzūra*," was all I offered.

MacShaka sniffed.

"Hoots. Ye'll no' hang the pettit lip over nothin', Sikunder," he chided unconvinced. "Speak yer mind, fer fuck sakes."

I finished my coffee, placed the cup on the table and pushed it away. "Today was just a bad day, *Huzūra*; nothing more really."

"Aye," MacShaka accepted with a nod. "It didnae gae the way I would hae wished. Jawans bein' shot is no' what I want tae hear about when I'm tryin' tae hae a bath, Sikunder."

"And I'm a little worried about Amina," I added almost under my breath.

"Aye," MacShaka empathized as he looked upon his hand, "She's taken it hard, bein' shot. Who wouldnae though? You," he said with a widening smile, "cried for your mither the whole time I was lookin' for a bullet hole in ye after ye'd been shot by the Black Hand. A dowie keelie ye were all because of a wee bullet wound. No even pierced yer Privnor armour, lad."

"It still hurt," I replied in wounded tones. The flesh was still tender below my collar bone six months later.

"Aye, it would," MacShaka retorted. "She'll gaet over it, I'm sure. Just takes time. Took you a few weeks tae get over getting yer wee hand cut up by the knife o' that Sindhi pirate tryin' tae kill ye on the *Naimaidan Regina* all o' those months back."

That Sindhi pirate trying to cut my throat, I thought. *"Breathe deeply, jawan, for it shall be your last."* It still sent shivers through me. Fortunately, MacShaka had cut him down with an axe before he had the chance to finish me.

"She'll be fine, Sikunder. Dinnae ye worry about her. Take a moment tae reflect on yerself, lad. Sindi pirate tried tae cut yer throat; shot by the Black Hand when ye went in with poor Fremantle Freya and her Gliesiuns, bless her soul; and charged up the beach and intae a Black Hand fort in Coloe Vallis. Look at ye now, after six months o' that. Back from two weeks wi' yer ain command herding cattle. Ye're what, still 17?"

"I'll be 18 next week," I replied.

"Aye," MacShaka said as he settled back. "Ye've come through alright. Gie' her the same time and she'll be fine as well," he finished in matter of fact tones. Now," he added, "ye should gae and sleep, yours will be a long enough day boakin' down the side o' yer camel and freezin' yer arse off. Teach you and that Greek for takin' matters intae yer ain haunds." With that, MacShaka stood, gave me one of his rare winks, and left the tent.

Well, I didn't feel quite so bad after that. A rare vote of confidence from him went a long way to making me feel a little bit better about my miserable lot in life.

* * * * *

The morning dawned gloomy with light snow falling. It was cold when Lukianos and I struggled through another few centimetres of new fallen snow to retrieve our tundra camels. After they were loaded with saddles, rations, and pulse rifles with 100 rounds per man, we mounted them and trotted out the gate towards the gathering column of the Constabulary.

I had been unsure what to expect when I woke up early that morning with Jindan handing me a cup of coffee and then laying out my uniform on my sleeping bag while I shivered in the darkness of the tent. I had gotten dressed quickly thereafter (already wearing long underwear, thank God!) pulling on *salwars*, *kameez*, *sherwani*, *chapan* coat and *postin*, two pair of wool socks and winter boots, tartan scarf, then webbing, crimson sash and 9mm pistol. I opted for the much warmer black turban, vice my *Pakol* beret, and when Jindan finished that off with the brass *sarpeesh* of Panthera Centuria and wrapped the tail around my face and throat, I felt I was indeed ready to face the world. When I meant to leave, however, Jindan grasped my hand.

"*Sirdar*," she said with that disarming smile, "you must never leave without your Khyber knife and hatchet."

They were heavy and bulky tucked into my sash, and I said so as I hissed at how much kit I was already carrying. Jindan brushed aside my complaints.

"*Sirdar*, have you never heard of *Huzūra* MacShaka's Rule of Nine?"

I hadn't, and knowing the brute was always dripping with Glaswegian wit and wisdom, I was surprised.

"MacShaka *bahadur* told me once, when he was on Gliesium, that he fought against the Gliesiuns when they breeched his castrum. He was with Havilders Cong and Sanghera Singh, fighting to the last man and the last bullet. He told me he watched a jawan fight to his last bullet and then die as he was cut down by a *barra* Gliesiun warrior from the *Athand'u* tribe. When MacShaka was surrounded and his pulse rifle empty, he too was left with his pistol. Eight bullets and he killed eight warriors. There was no ninth bullet for the ninth warrior that attacked him, so he fought hand-to-hand with the creature using his knife and hatchet. The knife and hatchet, *Sirdar*, is the Rule of Nine. Never leave without them; they may be all you have left in this world to prevent you from being sent to the next."

Well, I laughed it off as I tucked the weapons in my sash (while secretly dreading the thought of ever having to fight someone hand-to-hand with a Khyber knife and hatchet) and then with a very uncomfortable peck on the cheek from Jindan, I was out the tent door where Lukianos was waiting impatiently.

"You will need to decide what to do with that girl," Lukianos said in sage tones. "Do not lead her along if you are unwilling. Make up your mind. He who's hungry dreams of bread-loaves."

"Good God, Lukianos!" I replied with some shock. "She's just turned 16!"

"You are 17, Sikunder," he replied chuckling.

I put it out of my mind, though he had a point. I couldn't simply let it simmer. I didn't want to hurt her feelings – nor her to hurt my body – so the best thing would be a heart to heart with my havildar when I returned in the evening.

When Lukianos and I arrived at the bridge, the movement in the darkness was significant, and when I engaged my night vision contact lenses, I was thrilled with the sight of the column of horseman gathering in preparation for riding. I had expected a patrol the size of our contubernium, 10 or so, but the column that was forming had to be four times that if not more. Lukianos seemed as surprised as I, for he smiled and bade me follow him to see the Deputy Warden.

"The deputy is named Jasbinder Talib Singh, and he is a veteran of the Legion who lost his arm on Gliesium many years ago. Unlike every other army in the world where they would simply give you an artificial limb, the Legion simply releases you. He was given his 12 hectares for each of his years of service, and he resettled on Samsāra in Bryna Vallis. Bored of farming, however, he leased his lands and joined the Pavonis Constabulary seven years ago. I have known him for many years," Lukianos added with a nod of approval. "He is a fine deputy and a clever man."

We approached the column, still shrouded in the deep predawn darkness. Through the falling snow, I spied a plump, jolly-looking fellow minus his left arm barking out orders to the 20 constables around him.

"This is a one day march, daffadar; so no, we will not be bringing extra tea for the constables. They will have enough in their thermoses or they will go without!" This said to a sergeant apparently who was likely bothering him at the behest of his men. Talib Singh spied us as we trotted up, and a wide grin crossed his thickly bearded face. "Lukianos. You have brought me a fine *bahadur*, I see. Poor MacShaka does know what he is missing as we march out to show the locals that the *Chúsheng* will not be a threat."

"You have quite a number today, *Huzūra*," Lukianos observed. Talib Singh nodded.

"Yes, I will take all of my 20 constables from my detachment here and I have hired another 30 local levies as deputy constables for the day." He stood up in his stirrups and called out loudly, "Just as cold disappears by sitting beside the fire, so are sins destroyed in the congregation of saints!" There was much cheerful laughter from his constables and the hired guns. "It is important, after your actions yesterday," he continued with a wink, "that the *Chúsheng* know we are here for good and that their time has come to an end. The locals will be most happy to see this fine column crossing the Ceallach and entering the valley. We will go about 20 or so kilometres in, to the settlement of Svarga, population of about 400 or so, to show the flag, and then we will come home. The *Chúsheng* will bother us only if they dare."

Well, it sounded grand. The column exuded power and authority – the constables dressed in their black uniform of *salwars, sherwani* and *pakol* beret while the 30 hired levies were attired in a mess of clothing with each carrying an issued pulse rifle and crossbelts of power packs and ammunition. It was enough to strike terror into the bands of roving, ill equipped and ill armed villains more used to preying upon helpless settlers and refugees. I seriously doubted we would see even one of the bastards, and I said as much to Lukianos.

"You never know, Sikunder. Sniping is easy, though I believe Talib Singh will show no mercy to anyone who would bother us today."

With his column in line, Talib Singh gave the signal to move out and the 50 constables and hired deputies, with two chilly jawans on their tundra camels in tow, trotted across the narrow slatted bridge and into the hostile wilds of Gleann Ceallach.

* * * * *

The light flurries didn't stop. As the column shuffled through nearly 10 centimetres of snow, and the low glowering cloud darkened the valley while the temperature dropped to nearly -10 C, Lukianos and I shivered in our despondency knowing we wouldn't have the opportunities for warmth that the rest of the decuria would be enjoying, all thanks to some impetuous shooting by my Greek comrade. It was maddening, really, as I sipped hot tea from a thermos, pulled a heavy wool cloak from one of my saddle bags, and wrapped it around my shoulders. All this for shooting up a few criminals bent on mischief; it defied fairness. Lukianos was no happier as we pushed deeper into the gleann; he was sunk into his own cloak wrapped around his head and shoulders while the remainder of the column, so chatty initially, had fallen into silence. The cold was certainly dampening our spirits, but the solitude of our march, over a narrow trail between flanks of thick brooding forest, only made it worse.

Gleann Ceallach proper was several kilometres wide in places, but the path we travelled following the frigid cataracts of the Ceallach, already beginning to freeze for the long winter, was in an open meadow some 200 meters wide from tree line to tree line. Sometimes it closed to 100 meters and the deep brooding darkness beneath the canopy that held all manner of monsters and criminals, would crowd as close to us as 50 meters. It was disarming and kept me on edge. I felt like we were being watched with unknown eyes noting our slow plodding progress and our loss of cohesiveness as the terrain caused the column to open up. I was getting fidgety with anxiety, and I loosed my pulse rifle in its saddle holster.

But what could the *Chúsheng* do?

The first five or so kilometres had been the busiest with human habitation; several small settlements, farmsteads, yurts, log cabins, some travellers and merchants. It was hardly a buzzing metropolis of course, but we saw a number of settlers as they went about their daily grind. They drew water from the creeks and from the Ceallach, chopped wood, managed their livestock, and generally existed in what was about to become a six month deep freeze.

We paused on occasion to chat with the settlers who brought out pots of tea to warm us and to bathe in a certain relief at the power we represented. It gave me an opportunity to better see how they lived, and I wondered why they would take such chances in this isolated wilderness. One settlement we stopped at was a fine example of what we saw that day; a collection of rough cut wood shacks, yurts and outbuildings surrounded by an abatis wall of cut brush and branches. There were five families living there, a total of 36 Chinese refugees from a grandmother to a two month old girl. Between them, they held several hectares surrounding their homesteads and they worked the land in the summer planting crops for subsistence while they spent the off season clearing the forest or, when the weather imprisoned them, hunkered around a wood stove waiting for the months of frigid darkness to pass.

Their defences were meagre; the abatis wall, which would no more stop a bullet than a bulwark of sponges, would at least slow down someone from getting into their settlement. They had trade pulse rifles amongst them – cheaply built, low in power, and few in number – enough to keep the *Chúsheng* at bay and give them pause if they decided to take a slap at them for fun. For all of the danger around them, however, they seemed pretty happy with their lot, in large part due to the fact that they held nearly a square kilometre of land between them as their very own.

That was something beyond their wildest imagination on Earth.

As the morning wore on the number of individual settlements tapered off, and it was only on occasion that we would pass collections of buildings – small settlements of 50 people or less – as we proceeded deeper into the valley and further away from the castrum.

"I have been as far as the settlement of Svarga, about 20 kilometres in. It is a long march in weather like this," Talib Singh said to us as he brushed the snow from his beard, "but we can pause there for some tea. If it gets much worse," he added as he looked at the falling snow, "we can set up there for the night."

Spending the night was beginning to sound like an attractive option. One would have thought, here in 2098, that a weather report would have suggested that today was not a great day for a 40 kilometre trek to Svarga and back, but it appeared the meteorologists were getting it wrong.

"They called for no more than a few centimetres of snow today," Talib Singh groused. "No more. We have reached that already and it is not even noon."

We continued for another hour, and the disquiet I had been feeling increased. Too often I caught myself looking over my shoulder, and I soon realized I was not the only one. Although our hired guns seemed oblivious, most of the experienced constables were growing nervous, and Talib Singh, the veteran of the frontier and one, who supposedly owned the keen instinct of Kit Carson, was clearly concerned. When he finally raised his fist to order a halt, and the jangling of harnesses ceased, an eerie, terrible silence intruded. The breeze rolling down the valley, a soft keening, chilled me even deeper as the snowflakes billowed. I bade my tundra camel, Gomeda, move closer to Lukianos while I eased my pulse rifle from its holster.

"Something ain't right," I whispered. I couldn't credit it, whatever it was that was unnerving me and the troops around me. Our column, 52 pulse rifles in number, had to be the most powerful force 10 kilometres in any direction and yet, one could feel a palpable fear coming on. There was something out in the darkness of the lurking forest, some unnamed terror and it was hard to believe it could be the *Chúsheng*.

Lukianos pulled out his own rifle, as did many of the constables around us. As the column stood motionless, our eyes peered intently into the forest wall 100 meters to our left. Not a sound could be heard and not a movement could be seen; there was nothing to provoke the fear we felt save for the pervading silence.

"Daffadar," Talib Singh called out. "Take a position with 10 of the constables in the rear of the column. I will stay up here with the others and the two jawans. Put the hired deputies in the centre." He glanced at Lukianos and I and smiled; it lacked warmth and feeling. "It will make them feel safer."

"I'd like something to make me feel safer," I whispered to Lukianos. His greying face showed no response to my anaemic levity, which only made me feel worse. I powered up my pulse rifle and chambered a round. The sound made everyone around me jump, and Talib Singh allowed a thin smile. "The jawan is wise. Power up and load." The column was locked and loaded now and still we waited, wondering what the silence, and our fear of it, portended.

The Ceallach to our right was less than 25 meters away, its black waters sluggish in the cold. Beyond, the tree line was some 25 meters to the west though I could see a defile in the thick forest; a stream that flowed down the valley side and into the Ceallach. Beside it was a trail of sorts.

"What's up the valley?" I asked Talib Singh.

"The Artus Vallis? Just a convent," he grunted.

"A convent?" I repeated with obvious surprise

"The Nuns of St. Brigid," Lukianos said. He spat and looked peevish. "Their cardinal runs the place."

The Cardinal of Gleann Ceallach, I thought. That's where she lived.

"Any point in maybe heading up there?" I queried in an undertone. As much as I was fully aware of my failings in the courage department, I was hardly ready to broadcast it to the rest of the column.

"Sikunder," Lukianos replied with measured patience, "a servant of God fasts because he doesn't have any food. She would probably be of no help to us."

"Why not?" I asked with some surprise.

"Jesus, Sikunder..." but he got no further.

From the forest wall on our left came a sudden deep baying, like a thousand dogs howling wildly at the moon. "*Hooooooooom!*" was the sound that made me jump and cry out in shock. It was a terrible sound, full of malice and malevolence, and it grew in its depth and intensity over the next several seconds before dying off.

"Gliesiuns," Talib Singh muttered as he tapped the comm bud in his ear to call in the threat.

"Gliesiuns?" I asked as I looked at Lukianos. "What the hell?" But he ignored me, his jaw set and face grim. Suddenly the noise sounded again.

"*Hoooooooooooom!*"

It seemed to come from the entirety of the forest wall as if the very trees were alive with hate.

"That is their war cry," Lukianos said evenly.

The column was chattering, panicked at the threat. Horses bucked and tottered and even Gomeda seemed unnerved.

The singular, dreadful howl changed to a long low growl that began to build. It was a deep piercing resonance that seemed to shake the very ground as it grew in both volume and hatred. The constables were jabbering loudly, but Talib Singh and Lukianos were quiet and pale with fright.

"The *Nafrat*," Talib Singh murmured. He looked at me, his eyes widening in shock. "The Song of Hate."

"They are going to attack," Lukianos said breathlessly. "Oh my God."

Suddenly, figures spat from the shadows of the forest wall, sprinting through the snow with a speed that was astounding.

"Take them down!" screamed Talib Singh as he raised his pistol and fired.

There were many things that had terrified me on Samsāra; that frontal assault on the beach of the Coloe Vallis had been the worst. There was something intensely unnatural about jumping off the bow of a paddlewheeler and onto the rocky beach when hundreds of Black Hand bandits were firing upon us. The hell of that noise – recoilless rifle rounds exploding on the fascines, the piercing skirl of a dozen pipers from Gleann Fearadadh, the snap of fanning bullets, and the inhuman screams of the dying – had nearly finished me. I had survived it though, and mastered a paralyzing fear that would rarely plague me ever again. That day however, that moment as I gazed upon the horde of Gliesiuns emerging from the tree line 100 meters away, fear not only took me, but absolute panic overwhelmed me.

The creatures that sprinted towards us were *Athand'u* – I'd seen similar tribes before, like the *Ossayuln*; three meters in length, saurian in nature with long straight tails for balance, powerful hind legs, long forearms with three fingers, and a long equine head. Their heads were what horrified me – painted in their entirety in brilliant scarlet war paint with their eyes painted black into oversized and hideous sockets. Most wore a *caparison* of some kind over the short, coarse hair of their bodies, a thickly woven blanket, striped or checked, that ran from the base of their neck to the beginning of their tail. Some wore armour; *chamfron* masks with *rondel* spikes, segmented *crinets* on their necks, and mail *flanshards* on their sides. Others wore thick leather and mail *peytrals* over their narrow chests, and some even wore segmented *croupiers* down their backs and tails. It was their dyed scarlet heads though, against the alabaster blanket of snow, with mouths open in their terrible baying that had me near tears.

"Shoot, Sikunder!" Lukianos screamed as he fired. The *Athand'u* were armed with heavy long barrelled trade rifles that fired a massive 12mm bullet. These they fired on the run as they closed the distance to the column in seconds – the bullets buzzing amongst us like angry hornets and knocking down constables, hired deputies, and horses with equal ease. Gomeda bucked and staggered, and I saw the gaping bloody exit wound in his neck. He fell from beneath me, and I was suddenly on my back in the snow.

"Sikunder, get up and shoot!" Lukianos cried as he dropped off his own camel and fired.

I did as I was told, firing blindly at the springing creatures that were suddenly amongst the column. Once within our meagre defences, the *Athand'u* dropped their rifles and pulled out two meter long *lancea* staffs with serrated 30 centimetre blades on each end. These they swung and stabbed with a horrible precision, thrusting and slashing at the humans around them with a martial skill that was devastating. Screams filled the air, drowning out the sounds of gunfire. The deputies ran, dropping their pulse rifles and fleeing in a blind panic in every direction. The *Athand'u* made hideously short work of them as they hunted them down, slashed their necks and tore their heads off. Each death brought a bestial scream from the *Athand'u* before they turned to look for their next victim. I was barely functioning, so intense was my panic. I fired and fired, not even realizing my magazine was empty. Only when Lukianos punched me in the arm and told me to reload did I do so, pulling out another magazine to insert into my rifle with agonizing slowness before I recommenced firing.

I don't even know if I hit anything.

Individual memories stand out from those moments far better than the blurry whole that I recall now. Talib Singh trying to reload his pistol one handed while a shrieking *Athand'u* fell upon him with her *lancea*. The old warrior dropped the pistol, and pulled his *talwar* sword from his saddle.

"Death would not be called bad, O people, if one knew how to truly die!" he roared before the *Athand'u* stabbed the old deputy through the throat and then beheaded him; a pair of young Chinese deputies hired for the day, one missing a leg and the other his arm, laying amongst the slaughter of a trio of horses – "*Mŭqīn!* *Mŭqīn!*" "Mother! Mother!" they cried in their last moments alive; and Lukianos, his eyes filling with tears as he groped at his empty webbing searching for another magazine.

"Sikunder," he shrieked as he stood to run towards a pair of dead constables and their ammo belts, "run for the Ceallach! Cross it, boy, and hide in the trees!"

I didn't move for a moment, and Lukianos slapped me across the face. "Run, Sikunder! Please!" he added as he burst into tears. "Just run, boy! Run!"

I'm not proud of that moment – the moment I left my friend.

I won't defend that act of cowardice save to say that I was now in a full panic. The *Athand'u* were amongst us, hand-to-hand with the remains of the column, less than 20 people I suppose. I dropped my rifle and without looking back, ran for the dark waters of the Ceallach. It was snowing harder now which offered me a modicum of cover in the riotous melee. I plunged into the chilling river, waist deep, and pushed my way across before crawling up the far bank. The number of shots was fading, but the horrific screams were increasing. I didn't look back though to watch those final moments of the column, or of my friend Lukianos. Soaked and freezing, I ran through the snow until I entered the tree line, and even then I didn't stop moving and weeping until I came to the meandering stream called the Artus and its relative safety. I reached it finally, breathless, gasping and sobbing in horror.

I was alone with *Athand'u* all around me. I could not possibly survive.

I spied a series of deadfall logs across the stream, and a thought of safety penetrated the blind panic; I could shelter there, hide until help came. I stumbled towards the logs but spun around when I heard the malevolent shriek behind me.

The *Athand'u* was no more than a few meters away, crouched low, its hideous scarlet head bent close to the snow. Its arms were outstretched, one held a *lancea* dripping gore, the other, a small teardrop shaped *scutum* shield. The creature hissed, and I was mesmerized by its terrible eyes – irises of palest blue, almost reptilian and filled with hate. It took a step forward and I fumbled with the pistol on my belt.

The creature lunged and swung its *lancea* in a powerful backslash that missed me by a centimetre as I stumbled backwards and tripped. The *Athand'u* leapt over me, turned in a heartbeat and swung her *lancea* again, this time slapping the pistol from my hand with the flat of the blade and opening up my cheek to the bone. Again she hissed and swung. I ducked, but realized too late that she was using her tail on the back stroke, which caught me a powerful blow in the side. My ribs exploded in agony and I lay doubled over clutching my side and wheezing. Crying out in panic and agony, I tried to scramble to my feet but failed. I couldn't stand, so intense was the pain. I could only pull out my Khyber knife and crawl blindly towards those fallen logs and their tease of shelter as I waited for the creature to finish me.

But it didn't.

Unable to go any further, I rolled onto my back, gasping and sobbing as death approached, the tears rolling down my bloody cheek. I looked up and saw to my astonishment that the creature was prancing. It was a victory dance, a mocking hateful performance meant to humiliate me before she finished me off. She crowed and cooed, spun and leapt, and then slowly, provocatively, she stalked towards me. The *lancea* was raised as she straddled me with her powerful legs and lowered her hideous face to mine, barring her chiselled teeth and bathing me in her foetid breath. For a moment I held those monstrous pale eyes with mine – staring into my death. Then the *Athand'u* closed hers, for just a moment. Perhaps it was the rapture of the kill, but in that moment, I instinctively pulled the Khyber knife, which lay hidden in the snow, and thrust the 60 centimetre blade into her throat.

The *Athand'u* shrieked and fell back, pawing at the jutting knife before falling onto her side. I didn't spare her a second glance as I crawled towards that deadfall. The glacial water was piercing and it dulled the fire of my broken ribs. As I wriggled into the bitter cold of the muck beneath those trees and pulled myself mostly out of the water, I knew for a fact that though I may not have died at the hands of that *Athand'u*, I would definitely die of the cold. Already I could feel the last reserves of heat leaving me, and as the final lingering sounds of battle faded to an eerie penetrating silence, I weakly pulled my arms into my sheepskin *postin* to prolong the inevitability of my approaching death. I lay there shivering for a minute before I suddenly remembered my death song from nearly six months before. As I had lain in a bog after being shot those many months before, I sang the words that I had sung during a Blood Ceremony with a tribe of *Ossayuln* Gliesiuns only the day before.

> "*When I was a lad I served a term*
> *As office boy in an Attorney's Firm*
> *I cleaned the windows and I swept the floor*
> *And I polished up the handle on the big front door*
> *I polished up the handle so carefully*
> *That now I am the ruler of the Queen's Navy.*"

The agony of my broken ribs and slashed cheek faded. My eyesight grew dark and the sound of trickling water was dulled into silence. My consciousness faded through soft layers of greys, each deepening their shade, until finally it faded to black. For the second time in six months, I died in a muddy bog in the colony of Samsāra, some 20 light years from home.

Part Five
The Lonely House on the Hill

"The Lord is my shepherd, I shall not be in want. He makes me lie down in green pastures, he leads me beside quiet waters, he restores my soul. He guides me in paths of righteousness for his name's sake. Even though I walk through the valley of the shadow of death, I will fear no evil, for you are with me; your rod and your staff, they comfort me. You prepare a table before me in the presence of my enemies. You anoint my head with oil; my cup overflows. Surely goodness and love will follow me all the days of my life, and I will dwell in the house of the Lord forever."

"Am I dying?" I asked. The thin veils of consciousness, those dark shadows that had held me for so long in their cold and empty embrace, began to fade. As each thin Stygian veneer was removed, a dull, tawny light greeted my open eyes. The nothingness that had been a steady companion dissipated and a dull ache began to fill my side.

"No," replied a voice; deep, motherly, yet stern, "at least, praise Brigid, not today."

"That doesn't make me feel better," I responded, my voice slurred and drowsy. I closed my eyes, fighting the shadows that were growing again.

"Be strong with Saint Brigid and her mighty power. Put on the full armour of God so that you can take your stand against the devil's schemes. For our struggle is not against flesh and blood, but against the rulers, against the authorities, against the powers of this dark world and against the spiritual forces of evil in the heavenly realms."

There was a maddening pause, followed by the flip of a page and the creak of a chair. The woman cleared her throat and continued.

"*Therefore put on the full armour of God, so that when the day of evil comes, you may be able to stand your ground, and after you have done everything, to stand. Stand firm then, with the belt of truth buckled around your waist, with the breastplate of righteousness in place, and with your feet fitted with the readiness that comes from the gospel of peace. In addition to all this, take up the shield of faith, with which you can extinguish all the flaming arrows of the evil one. Take the helmet of salvation and the sword of the Spirit, which is the word of God. And pray in the Spirit on all occasions with all kinds of prayers and requests. With this in mind, be alert and always keep on praying for all the saints.*"

I heard the gentle closing of a book.

"Where am I?" I asked as I fought to open my eyes and wrestle with the fleeting light of consciousness.

"Pacatus," explained the voice. It was grave and severe. "You are in Pacatus."

"Where's Pacatus?"

"Artus Vallis," the voice answered. "It is a small vallis of Gleann Ceallach. The Narrow Dale is the rough translation. Pacatus is about three kilometres up the stream. A little steep and slippery this time of year, so it was hard for us to carry you. But clearly we did," she finished with an indelicate hint at the trouble I'd caused for her.

I again opened my eyes. The room was cold and dark save for a single guttering candle on the table beside me. A musty smell greeted me, like old cut lumber and earth. The walls of the tiny room were rough hewn planks with bark edges while the wall at my head was barked trunks with mud and wattle filling the chinks. The ceiling was slanted and steep with straw and thin dangling roots piercing the seams. From the tall joists hung vegetables and dried herbs, bunches of onions, garlic, potatoes in the corner, mint, oregano, basil, and rosemary – a green grocer with myself deposited in the middle.

I was in the convent, I presumed, the one Talib Singh had told me about with the nuns and their mysterious cardinal.

A woman sat in a chair by the bed. She was older, perhaps mid 60s. Her head was shaved save for a thin braided topknot of silver hair that fell down her back. She was a small woman, narrow waisted though it was difficult to tell beneath the bulk of the deep blue homespun cassock and black scapular on her shoulders. The face was tight lipped and severe, though the deep brown eyes were somewhat at odds with the dour facade. They were hard, flinty, yet one could discern a certain sympathetic quality in them.

"Who are you?" I asked. My voice was a mere croak, for the pain in my side that had begun with subtle suggestion was growing more insistent.

"My name is Reverend Mother Mary Margaret," she replied. She had a light English accent – West Country perhaps. She sniffed and added, "Though I dare say you've heard some refer to me as the Cardinal of Gleann Ceallach."

"I've heard of you," I returned as I struggled to sit up. The pain made me gasp and she placed a firm hand on my chest and pressed me back down onto the narrow bed.

"Don't sit up. You've done enough foolishness for one day, jawan," she said in a harsh rasp. "You've several fractured ribs and that's quite a gash on your face. We've put a bio-dressing on it, but moving around and talking to excess will only slow the healing."

I lay there trying to make sense of my situation; the last moments before I blacked out – the horrors of the ambush, the fight by the stream, and then nothing.

"Lukianos," I whispered as a sudden surge of emotion ran through me. "What happened to Lukianos?"

"The other jawan?" Coulthard asked as she placed her Bible on the table. "I regret to say that he did not survive." She moved and gripped my hand and said, "*Bless those who mourn, Saint Brigid, with the comfort of your love, that they may face each new day with hope, and the certainty that nothing can destroy the good that has been given. May their memories become joyful, their days enriched with friendship, and their lives encircled by your love. Amen.*"

I closed my eyes to the tears. The guilt was terrible, for I had left someone behind. Lukianos and I had shared a few adventures in my six months on Samsāra, and although I couldn't count him as a close confidante, he was my comrade in arms and when I was most needed by him, I turned my back and fled. She patted my hand.

"I'm not sure how you ended up where you did, jawan," Coulthard said, "but punishing yourself for it will not do."

I wiped my nose and eyes. "I left him behind," I blubbered. New tears rolled down my cheeks. "He told me to run and I did. I left him behind." I felt sick and thought I would vomit.

"It was a noble thing he did," Coulthard consoled after a long pause. She patted my hand once more and then sat back in her chair, queenly and severe. "What do you think you will accomplish by feeling guilty about that gift?"

"Gift?" I sobbed, for I was absolutely falling apart now.

"Yes, jawan, gift," she replied in a harsh, lecturing tone. "Your friend gave you the gift of life, or at least, he gave you the gift of a chance at life. You were fortunate. Now, you sully such generosity by feeling guilty about it. Remember what I said in my prayer? *Face each new day with hope, and the certainty that nothing can destroy the good that has been given.* The good that was given to you by your friend was his sacrifice so that you might have a chance to survive."

"I ran," I repeated.

"He told you to," she replied with infinite patience though her voice maintained its cutting edge. "He made his decision and offered you a chance. What should you have done? Refuse such complete generosity and die beside him? What would that have accomplished?" She crossed her arms and looked upon me in disapproval. "Generosity and sacrifice do not exist, jawan, if no one benefits from them. You both would have simply died, and no memory or honouring of such an act would occur." She paused to cross herself. "*And if I give all my possessions to feed the poor, and if I surrender my body to be burned, but do not have love, it profits me nothing.*"

I didn't credit it at the time, as she patiently explained what Lukianos had done, but in hindsight, I grew to understand that his gift, given so freely, could not be turned down, at least, not without negating the sacrifice. Then, however, I couldn't see it. I felt far too horrible. Finally, as I wiped away the tears and sought to control my shattered emotions I asked, "Does my decuria know what happened?"

"Yes," Coulthard replied after pause. She crossed her legs beneath her voluminous cassock. "When we heard the shooting, we went down to investigate. By the time we arrived, it was over. The *Athand'u* were gone and we only found you because one of the sisters walking near the stream heard you moaning. We found you and brought you back to the convent."

"How long?"

"You have been here for 12 hours," she replied after a glance at her watch.

"My decuria left me here?" I didn't know if I should be furious or horrified at the seeming lack of interest.

"Don't be foolish, jawan," she replied with an edge. She focused her deep brown eyes on me. "You have fractured ribs and were hypothermic. You were in no shape to travel and frankly you are quite safe here. Your subedar, Motshegwa, said it was best if you stayed here until the weather broke anyway. It has not stopped snowing. It is not safe in such weather," she finished grimly.

"Safe," I repeated as I relived the horror of the ambush. "How could it be safe with the Gliesiuns anyway?"

"The *Athand'u* are a peaceful tribe," she lectured as she leaned back in her chair and crossed her arms again. "If they attacked you, they must have felt provoked."

"Peaceful?" I returned. The image of the *Athand'u* warrior poised to slash me did not seem to fit with her notion of peaceful. "They ambushed us."

"They did," she agreed. "I am curious to know why."

The door to my room opened and I suddenly felt myself go white and my heart pound until I thought it would explode. From the darkness of the doorway emerged a shape – morphing from the shadow into the sphere of thin ochreous light. A Gliesiun carrying a pitcher and cup in one three fingered hand and a towel in the other; it looked exactly like an *Athand'u*. It took every effort not to shriek and thrust myself under my blankets.

"Calm yourself, jawan," Coulthard said in a stern voice. "This is sister Caelina Junia. She has brought you water."

The Gliesiun paused beside my bed and placed the towel at my feet. Its hideous pale blue eyes in its equine head were fixed on me as it poured water into a cup before placing it on the table beside my bed.

"*Laudetur Jesus Christus*, Sister Caelina," Coulthard said by way of thanks.

The Gliesiun named Caelina bobbed and muttered thickly, "*In sæcula*."

I had never heard a Gliesiun speak a human tongue, even if it was Latin, and it shocked me. The voice was heavy and guttural like gravel spread with a rake, the words slurred and barely understandable. Coulthard dismissed the creature with a wave.

"Caelina is one of three Gliesiun sisters, all from the *Athand'u*. I have the other two linking up with the tribe to determine what it was that caused this event."

"You mean massacre," I interjected as my heartbeat, barely coming down, began to rise again. "There were 52 constables, jawans, and deputies out there for a one day patrol, sister. Show the flag," I groused, "nothing more. Go to Svarga, pause for lunch, and return. Everyone sleeps in their own cot and everyone lives. Not now," I finished hotly. "Now there's 51 dead people in the snow along with a bunch of your peaceful *Athand'u* lying beside them."

"Calm yourself, jawan," Coulthard snapped. As much as her voice was harsh, there was a softening in her deep piercing eyes.

She had me fired up now with her nonsense. Peaceful were they? Screaming like banshees as they burst amongst us; slashing and shooting. It was a horrific slaughter that had cost me a comrade, and some nun had the temerity to brush it aside like it was some playground misunderstanding. Not likely!

For several moments we endured an angry silence, then she handed me the glass of water. "Drink, jawan," she commanded in a soft voice.

I did and felt better for it. I'm not sure why she felt compelled to stay, but she seemed eager for conversation and she steered it away from recent events as she sought to sooth my shattered emotions. "What is your name?"

I gave her my name, background, and a précis of my last six months on Samsāra. She nodded as I explained the sordid tale of my running away from home and my recent announcement to my parents about my fate nearly nine months after disappearing one February evening. It occurred to me then that my parents had once again come close to receiving some institutional explanation of my death by beheading or freezing to death in an obscure little valley named Gleann Ceallach, in the colony of Samsāra, some 20 light years from Earth.

For all of my pique at her apparent indifference to the men and women who had just died, I must admit a burgeoning curiosity at her circumstances. I was not in the castrum long enough to hear more than a bit of gossip about this intriguing woman and her followers but I now had the opportunity to slake the thirst of my interest. "And you," I muttered. "How does a convent come to be built here?"

Coulthard glanced at her watch. "A few more minutes," she answered, "then you must rest. This convent has been here for five years," she began. She paused as the Gliesiun re-entered and I once again fought panic and a rising rage. This time the creature brought in a cup of tea and placed it on the table. "*Gratius*, Caelina. *Non aliud requiro.*"

"She speaks Latin?" I asked.

Coulthard picked up her cup and stirred it languidly. After tapping the spoon, she placed it on the table beside the saucer. "Yes. She speaks it after a fashion. Her tongue and lips don't allow her to enunciate very well, however. Now, where was I? Right, a convent in Artus Vallis." She sipped her tea, sat back in her chair and continued.

"We built this convent five years ago when only a handful of families had settled here. It was remote yet still within a couple of days of the Seleucus Lacus. Agarum had not even been begun then, only a pair of families had built cabins and were fishing. It started off as a yurt but grew as more followers came. Most are poor refugee women who have lost their families, or they were young girls we rescued from brothels and others forms of slavery in Ophir. Men are not allowed here, though as you can see," she said as she spared me a cool glance, "they can be welcomed as guests."

The candle flickered as a breeze pierced the wall. It was freezing in the room and I huddled under my blankets.

"This building we have constructed over the years," Coulthard continued as her eyes wandered around the darkened room. She reached out to touch the rough wall. "It serves us and allows the sisters to pray, reflect, and prepare in order to go out and help in the colony. Those who prefer a quiet solitude are as welcome. I do not judge them." Abruptly she stood and gathered the thick woollen cassock around her slender frame. "Now, jawan, you need your rest. You will sleep for now and in the morning you must eat. We will see how you feel. The bad weather is predicted to last at least another 24 to 48 hours, so we may be your only company for a while."

With that, she bent down and blew out the candle. The darkness was penetrating and terrifying. As I felt a dreadful panic begin to rise, I heard her soft chanting, "*Brigid is my light and my salvation; whom shall I fear? Brigid is the strength of my life; of whom shall I be afraid? When the wicked, even mine enemies and my foes, came upon me to eat up my flesh, they stumbled and fell. Though a host should encamp against me, my heart shall not fear: though war should rise against me, in this will I be confident.*"

Her voice faded as she exited the room and closed the door. I felt somewhat relieved; enough at least to fall asleep.

* * * * *

I woke up the following morning with a cat on my feet. The room was dark, though thin slivers of milky light pierced the unfilled chinks in the wall behind my headboard, one of which illuminated the soft fur of a sleeping calico cat. The creature was bundled in wool blankets and thin vapourous clouds emanated from its mouth. When I breathed, it was the same, for the room was dreadfully cold – well below freezing, as the frozen water in my glass attested. I moved my feet slowly and the cat awoke to spare me a piercing scowl for daring to disturb her.

"Sorry," I whispered. I didn't like cats, but there was something in this creature's damn-your-eyes look that demanded a degree of servility from me. I had to pee and decided I couldn't hold it any longer. When I moved, the pain of my fractured ribs intruded and I gasped, which made it worse. I sat for a moment, my hand on my side as I fought through a wave of dizziness. After a brief time in which the cold penetrated my woollen long underwear, I searched for my clothes in the darkness with its few narrow beams of light, and spied them on a chair in the corner. Gritting my chattering teeth, I eased my way out of the fleeting warmth of the bed and into the frigid air of the room.

"Holy shit," I stuttered as I loped over to the chair and pulled on my *salwars* and *kurta*. I had two pairs of wool socks, thankfully dry; a thick wool sweater; *sherwani* and *chapan*; and finally my *postin* vest. Boots and then my turban – ham-fisted and misshapen as it was. It took me a few minutes. By the time I was done, I was feeling hypothermic again and as I shivered the excruciating pain in my ribs was made worse. Grabbing gloves and my thick woollen Royal Stewart tartan scarf, I exited my room into a narrow hall lit by a single lamp. There were doors to other small rooms on either side and one opposite mine a few meters ahead. I crept along wincing with each step and unsure of the time, I had lost my watch in the fight, I hoped not to disturb anyone. When I opened the door it revealed a large open room the width of the building, about 10 meters or so and some 10 meters in length, filled with rough pine bunk beds; all of which were empty.

"Hello?" I whispered.

"Meow," was the reply as I looked at the cat rubbing against my boot. It purred, rubbed its whiskers on the filthy cracked Gortex, and moved off towards another door as if leading me. Figure that, I thought as I followed. Even a cat could take charge of me. I passed through the door and into another hallway of creaking floorboards with stairs going down. I followed the cat as it padded through the darkness and down the stairs. The room below was a common room with a stone fireplace and a roaring fire throwing out inviting heat. I paused there, as did the cat, and enjoyed the warmth. I noted a door nearby with hints of snow and mud at its sill that ran as a trail to a wood bin beside the fireplace. I opened it and had to step back from the brilliance that met me.

It was full on morning with snow continuing to fall lightly. The exit opened onto a courtyard, a dazzling alabaster space about 20 meters squared. At the far end, the courtyard opened through a set of double gates to the vallis and forest beyond while the convent itself rose two rough, wooden stories around me in a building 40 meters squared. There were several cloaked figures in the courtyard, thickly robed against the cold temperatures – for it must have been near - 10 degrees – shovelling snow and uncovering cords of firewood. It was the object dominating the centre of the courtyard that held me in thrall, however, for thrusting through a deck five meters square was a towering crude wooden statue carved from a single Pavonis pine trunk – a slightly bowed feminine figure in hooded robes with hands resting upon the hilt of a downturned sword. The face, as brutish as the carving was, held my attention. A solemn face, peaceful and reposed, yet with determined eyes open to the terrible threat of the world.

It was Saint Brigid; a frightfully pagan, Old Testament, eye-for-an-eye, tooth-for-a-tooth, hellfire and brimstone, Saint Brigid,

At each corner of the deck stood a nun, each with her face hidden deep within her heavy hooded cassock, swinging a thurible of smoking incense – made from Pavonis pine resin and a particularly fragrant, local stonecrop rose, if I recall correctly – and chanting in Latin. It translated roughly to:

"O Victorious Brigid!
Thou who has ever such powerful influence
in conquering the hardest of hearts,
intercede for those for whom we pray,
that their hearts being softened
by the rays of Divine Grace,
they may return to the unity of the true Faith."

I wasn't sure what to make of it all, for the final accessory carried by the four nuns, that caused me to raise an eyebrow in surprise, was a Khyber knife tucked into a sash wrapped around each of their waists. A most un-Christian of objects, I thought.

Then again, as I was to find out, the nuns of Saint Brigid were an unusual kind of Christian.

"I see you are awake," said a soft, high voice from within a deep woollen cowl. A figure walked through the snow to stand before me. "*The steadfast love of Brigia never ceases; her mercies never come to an end; they are new every morning,*" she chanted as she pulled back the cowl of her woollen cloak. Vaporous breath came from her nose as she smiled in greeting. "Would you like a cup of tea, jawan?" she asked in near perfect English.

The nun was in her teens I suspected, a young Chinese girl with head shaved and a pretty face marked by deep scars that left one eye closed. It took every effort not to react to that beaming face so badly damaged, so I smiled and nodded.

"Please."

"You may stay here or come. Reverend Mother Mary Margaret is out with a group clearing the trail to Gleann Ceallach."

"A bathroom would be nice," I said.

"Through that door," she said as she pointed towards a door opposite. "I will have your tea and some bread in the common room when you return."

The bathroom was an experience – a simple compost pit toilet after a fashion with no running water save what you dumped into it. When I returned to the common room and its blazing fire, the nun was standing beside a table with a cup of tea and a plate of black bread. "Your breakfast, jawan," she said with a charming smile. I took a seat and reached for the bread, but held off as the nun bowed her head, brought her tiny hands together and prayed.

"Dear Brigid, Thank you for preparing this table before us.
Thank you for the bounty of the earth,
which nourishes our bodies.
Thank you for the abundance of your goodness,
which sustains our lives,
strengthening us to serve you more effectively.
Thank you for the hands that prepared this meal
and for the joy of being able to share it.
For all we have received and all that is yet to come, Brigid,
we are thankful."

I nodded uncomfortably beneath her gaze, flashed a pained smile of appreciation for her spiritual ministrations, and began to eat cautiously as the pain in my side was growing worse. I kept my hand there, holding the taped ribs as I chewed and sipped tea. "What is your name?" I asked between mouthfuls.

"Sister Mei-ling," she replied with a small bow. "Reverend Mother Mary Margaret asked me to watch out for you until she returned."

"I appreciate that," I replied as I chewed the thick slices of black bread. The pain was growing; eating was making it worse.

"Your ribs," she observed as she pointed towards my hand. "I will get you some medicine for the pain."

I ate in silence as she left, kept company by the cat that had reappeared at my feet. When I was finishing my tea, she returned with a small glass of liquid.

"Drink this, it will help."

"When will the Reverend Mother return?" I asked after I drank the clear amber liquid. It had a slight brandy taste and was quite pleasant. I was restless for answers, and was eager to leave for the castrum.

"Soon," Mei-ling answered. "Do you wish to rest?"

"No," I replied. I got up, stiff and wincing, "I'd like to stretch my legs."

"I will take you for a walk around the convent, though the snow is high. We have had over 40 centimetres now and it is still snowing. It will take some time to clear the trail."

The walk was a slow one and much harder work than I likely should have done. Though a wide path had been cleared around the perimeter of the convent, the blizzard was still falling with no sign of letting up. We shuffled through the snow, avoiding the dozen or so sisters with shovels who were working constantly to keep a path clear. Others were carrying wood from large tarped stacks of cordwood into the courtyard where it was restacked for ready use. Few of these nuns spared me a glance as they worked though I had the opportunity to appraise them. They varied in age and nationality – some were girls as young as 10 while others were in their 80s. All were dressed in the same homespun woollen cassocks, their heads shaved save for their topknot – which I supposed was a badge of their time as nuns for some had none while others had extensive braids – and all worked with quiet diligence except for one who merely walked amongst them chiming out sonorous prayers and incantations as food for thought.

"*Great You are, O Brigid,*" the nun announced as she paused beside four other nuns stacking cordwood, "*and greatly to be praised; great is Your power, and Your wisdom is infinite. You would we praise without ceasing. You call us to delight in Your praise, for You have made us for Yourself, and our hearts find not rest until we rest in You; to whom with the Father and the Holy Spirit all glory, praise, and honour be ascribed, both now and forevermore. Amen.*" At another point, as she stood beside a pair of young nuns melting buckets of snow over a wood fire in the courtyard she recited, "*O Brigid, be present with us always, dwell within our hearts. With thy light and thy Spirit guide our souls, our thoughts, and all our actions, that we may teach thy Word, that thy healing power may be in us and in thy church universal. Amen.*"

Perhaps the most surprising moment came as we stood by the open gates looking upon the narrow vallis now obscured by the falling snow. The convent was built near the creek on an open *maidan* which had been further opened with the removal of some of the forest in the building of the convent. The forested hatchet slash of the vallis rose tall on either side while the stream and accompanying trail meandered downward, not too steep, towards Gleann Ceallach some three kilometres below. As I gazed upon the difficult location they had chosen to build, a nun turned the corner, and a thrill of shock passed through me when I noted she had a pulse rifle hanging off her shoulder and two crossbelts of webbing for magazines and power packs over her cassock. She paused for a moment to examine me with dark piercing eyes before moving on.

When she and the invoking nun met, they paused, bowed, and the invoking nun said in a pretty sing song voice, "*We give thanks to thee, omnipotent, everliving Brigid of truth, Sustainer of all things, Giver of all life, order, courage and wisdom, unfailing Source of help.*" When she finished, the well armed nun carried on her foot patrol and I was left more confused than ever.

"I'll think I'll go back and lie down for a while," I murmured, feeling very groggy. The pain had faded, masked by the drug that they had given to me. Mei-ling led me back to my room; helped me undress, for by now I could barely keep my eyes open; and tucked the blankets around me.

"Reverend Mother Mary Margaret will see you after you rest. Until then, you will have Querela to keep you company."

I felt the cat once again at my feet, thanked Mei-ling for her comfort, and allowed sleep to overcome me.

* * * * *

"Why are you armed?" I asked while trying to shake the grogginess from my mind with a bowl of soup. The common room was full for supper, some 50 or more nuns speaking in low whispers while the fire threw out heat and the earthy smell of the room was augmented by the aromas of mutton stew and fresh black bread.

Coulthard sat across from me; the sleeves of her cassock hoisted so that she could break bread and eat her stew without making a mess of her clothing. She paused and looked at me curiously – as if I'd farted or asked for a glass of Merlot.

"Do you think it would be wise to live here, a day's ride from the closest constabulary outpost, surrounded by the *Chúsheng*, and remain unarmed?" She seemed almost amused by the stupidity of the question – almost. "How long do you think we would last if that were the case, Sikunder?" A small smile crossed her tight lips. "The *Chúsheng* tried that very thing about two years ago. A score of them attacked us, ignorant of our ability to protect ourselves. Not a single one survived."

I was shocked, so much so that I dropped my spoon. Embarrassed, I picked it up and asked in quiet undertones, "You killed them all?"

"Of course," Coulthard replied, as if stating some obvious fact, like snow falls in winter, or that the Maple Leafs didn't stand a chance in this year's NHL playoffs. "The *Chúsheng* are not happy that we are here, and they kill off my nuns whenever they have the chance. If they are foolish enough to cross us, then they must suffer for it. *Blessed be Brigid, my rock,*" she droned in what was becoming a familiar militant dirge, "*Who trains my hands for war, And my fingers for battle; My loving kindness and my fortress, My stronghold and my deliverer; My shield and She in whom I take refuge; Who subdues my people under me.*" She crossed herself and resumed, "It would be the height of folly, Sikunder, not to be well armed even as we welcome the downtrodden and the broken. We are a beacon for them and we will protect them if they offer themselves to Brigid and God."

"Isn't it wrong?" I asked, even though I had a feeling that I knew what the answer would be. "I mean, you being nuns and all."

"Wrong?" Coulthard retorted with the sudden mien of an old timey Baptist evangelist. "What is wrong in defending yourself, Sikunder?"

"Well, nothing," I replied taken aback by the venom, "if you're a jawan or a cop. You're nuns, though."

"Yes," she countered primly as she unfolded a napkin and dabbed her lips. She pointed to her chin as an indication that I was an awful mess. "Tidy yourself, Sikunder," she chastened as she refolded her napkin. "This may be a convent in a tiny vallis on Samsāra, 20 light years from Earth, but it doesn't mean we eat like cattle nor do we exercise the manners of goats."

"Yes, ma'am," I bobbed, dabbing at my chin with my napkin. I fought the urge to stick my pinkie out when I reached for my tea – I had no doubt that she either had a ruler or a bullwhip tucked within her cassock.

"Yes, we are nuns, and proper Christians as well, Sikunder, if that is what you are hinting at. Dedicating ourselves to Brigid and God does not eliminate the need to defend ourselves. Turning the other cheek is very well when arguing with the idiocy of an atheist, Sikunder, but when they are trying to kill you, a cut throat serves your interest much better. We have not survived in a hostile vallis this long relying upon good will and miracles," she added in a severe undertone. "Brigid requires us to take care of ourselves as much as care for those around us. If that means a cost of blood, then so be it."

I was horrified. Within this grandmotherly abbess – aged and meek appearing as she entered her dotage – beat the heart of a Blood and Iron warrior. I couldn't credit it as I sat and listened to her wax Sun Tzu as she pointed out the strategies behind her stance, but the more she lectured the more I was sure she was somewhat touched in the head as well.

Coulthard looked grim as she spread a pat of butter on her bread. "*A time to love, and a time to hate; A time for war, and a time for peace*, Sikunder. We are the only force for good in this world, true goodness uncorrupted by greed, avarice, incompetence, and hate. We feed those who are hungry, heal those who are sick, defend those who are defenceless. The *Chúsheng* rarely bother us now except when they catch my nuns unaware, which is not often. I have been fortunate this year, I have only lost four; one of our better years."

"Four?" It was shocking to think that these nuns were a regular target as they transited between Pacatus and the rest of the colony.

"Of course," Coulthard exclaimed. Her dour visage returned. "Our work to help those who need help demands sacrifice. That we owe only allegiance to Brigid and not to the Company, the Legion, the Constabulary, nor any of the petty thugs and criminals of this colony makes us a terrible threat that cannot be controlled. It is simply better to kill us off when the opportunity arises."

Well, I didn't understand that and said so. Coulthard shrugged off my question and pointed towards Mei-ling. "You met sister Mei-ling this morning. She is 16 years old. I bought her from a brothel four years ago after she had been working in it since the age of nine. Two years ago, when she was helping newly arrived refugees in the camps east of Ophir, she was jumped by a pair of thugs and beaten nearly to death before they spent a night raping her. Why you might ask? Simply because she was there and willing to help protect the new arrivals from falling into the clutches of the gangs and criminal elements. They seek to recruit new members from the refugees and settlers. For us to survive there is a need to fight. Some will fight by simply resisting the evil urges that hold sway while others will raise a pulse rifle and put a bullet into a killer."

I found this fascinating – a collection of fighting nuns – yet it disturbed my stereotypical view of ruler wielding nuns in wimples. "How many would fight?" I asked.

"If needed," Coulthard replied after a moment's pause, "I could raise 50 rifles from the nuns, maybe more. One of the many reasons the *Chúsheng* will not bother us in force."

"Nor the Gliesiuns," I replied with some wonder at it all.

"The Gliesiuns have not shown much interest in conflict until yesterday, Sikunder," Coulthard lectured. "They have come here and existed quite peacefully, even with the *Chúsheng* though that is mostly because there is little to cause conflict between those two groups. We have worked well in the past with the *Athand'u*, *Ossayuln* and *Tasyage*, and *Ech'cha*. Something has changed, however, and I hope to find out what soon."

Something had changed. The Gliesiun tribes in Gleann Ceallach had taken an extraordinary step in their relations with the Constabulary and the Legion. The massacre, I expected, was making headlines on this world and at home with the likelihood that Legion and Constabulary ire was about to be unleashed. I said something to that effect and Coulthard sniffed in derision at my musing.

"Sikunder," she insisted after a moment of contemplating me. It felt like she was studying some lower life form, like a slug or a Montreal Allouettes fan. "Have you ever heard of *Volk Bashnya*?"

I had not and said so. Coulthard broke off a piece of bread and popped it in her mouth. After a moment of consideration she mused, "*Volk Bashnya* is a stone tower located at the top of the Lyaksandr Porta at the eastern entrance to Ilken Vallis just north of Ophir. It was built about 10 years ago by the Neo Cossacks under Hetman Vasyl Kosmenka – there is a maniac the Legion and Constabulary should have removed many years ago," she added with a hiss. "The tower was not much to look at really, wooden and stone palisades around a two-story, dry-stone monument to some foolish notions of Neo Cossack romanticism.

However, the Lyaksandr Porta can only be achieved after climbing nearly 500 meters from the vallis floor in the Himera Vallis up to the Lezviye Britvy ridge along a very narrow and difficult trail. At the best of times it is onerous, but when, six years ago, the Company grew weary of Neo Cossack depredations in its bioengineering lands in Schüssel Vallis to the east, everyone discovered just how much more difficult that trail could be made." She sipped her tea while I hung on her every word.

"Klondikecorp was not happy with the Neo Cossacks stealing its bioengineered mammoths and prehistoric rhinos from the Schüssel Vallis animal preserves so it pressured both the Constabulary and the Legion to put an end to it. Reluctantly, the Constabulary raised a force of 30 constables, dragooned the Legion into supplying 20 jawans, and hired over 50 deputies from the newly arrived refugees in the camps outside of Ophir. Everyone was afraid of a frontal move into Ilken Vallis for the pass from the western entrance, though deemed physically easier to enter, was very well defended. So as stealthily as they could, they moved the column into Himera Vallis from the south and attempted to move into Ilken Vallis from the east. As you can imagine, Sikunder, moving a column of over 100 soldiers and constables by truck south from Ophir into Albor Vallis in order to then march north through the trackless lands of Elaver Vallis and into Himera Vallis all without being detected was impossible. When the column achieved the summit of Lezviye Britvy and the Lyaksandr Porta, the Neo Cossacks were waiting in force at their tower. The battle lasted less than an hour before the column was sent in panic back down the trail. If memory serves, 17 constables, five jawans, and 18 deputies were killed that day. Only two Neo Cossacks died and neither the Constabulary nor the Legion has ever tried that foolishness again." She paused to sip her tea and I took the opportunity to interrupt.

"I'm not sure what this really has to do with the actions of the *Athand'u*."

"The point of this story, Sikunder," Coulthard continued with a cool damn your manners stare, "and remove your elbows from the table, by the way, is that 40 people died that day fighting for Klondikecorp. I went to Earth two weeks later to settle the affairs of my mother who had died, and as much as I scoured the news outlets to discover the fallout of this terrible massacre, I found nothing. In short, Sikunder, no one cared then, and I highly doubt anyone will care now. These events happen on a UN colony 20 light years from Earth and it is populated mostly by the poorest and meanest of refugees from the United Nations camps in Afghanistan, Tajikistan, and Uzbekistan. The constables, deputies, and jawan who died yesterday are the poorest of untrained and uncared for soldiers and police. No one cares what happened to you yesterday. So thoughts that the media is ablaze with tales of horror because of some massacre in Gleann Ceallach are unfounded. Even if it made it into a data transfer pack to be transmitted through the next opening of the hypergate, the media will not pick up on it. That's the simple sad fact here."

She was right of course. Years after, when I searched for references to that horrible day, I found little more than a few passing institutional memoirs describing the events that had passed that morning. Nothing more than a casual mention of facts and figures, and not a single name. Not Deputy Warden Talib Singh, not jawan Lukianos Kondylis, nor even Julia Hajdari, a young Albanian girl who had signed up to the constabulary at the age of 16 only days before, but who had actually only turned 14. There was nothing to recall to the world that these people had died in the service of Klondikecorp and of the United Nations; a sad testimonial to the throw away existence of these people.

I spent the rest of the evening resting in the warmth of the common room in a chair near the fire, doped up as I was on laudanum (that was the liquid given to me earlier by Mei-ling apparently) with the cat named Querela on my lap. With a cup of milky tea by my side and the shadows of the room flickering by the light of the fire, I mused upon one of my more fascinating days on Samsāra.

The Nuns of Saint Brigid; I hadn't heard of them before. I suspected, however, that they were a curious offshoot – a certain kind of evolutionary abomination that the Catholic Church was loathe to acknowledge or give any form of credence to. These nuns weren't alone of course, for I'd heard of the Monks of Saint Andrew in Tajikistan, the Soldiers of Saint George in Afghanistan, and of course, the legendary Death Angels of Saint Michael located in the Hindu Kush. Each was a curiously militant group of fanatical warriors who had moved beyond the restrictive bounds of Christ's turn the other cheek teachings to a club the hell out of them fire and brimstone of old, and it was tacitly understood that they were well supplied with weapons and training to carry out their bloody work. These nuns seemed to follow a similar vein, though from what little I'd seen, they lacked the support that other groups had in spades.

I sat there groggy and brooding for an hour at least before Mei-ling appeared. She smiled and bowed, then brought her dainty hands together in prayer.

> "*Saint Brigid, may Your peace and mercy enter into this house
> along with my humble entrance.
> Let every wickedness of the devil flee from this place.
> May the angels of peace be here,*

and may every sinful discord leave this home.
Show that Your name is great among us, O Brigid,
and bless our living together.
Brigid, You are holy and faithful, and You remain with the Father
and the Holy Spirit for ever and ever, Amen."

"It is time for you to go to bed, Brother Sikunder," she said in the sweet tiny voice so at odds with her hideous face.

"I'm not really tired," I slurred as I tried to wave her away. She would not be brushed off, however.

"Reverend Mother Mary Margaret would be displeased if you were to spend the night here and not in your room," she giggled as she helped me stand. For her elfin size, she was surprisingly strong. "Come, Brother Sikunder, I will help."

It was slow progress as I staggered. Mei-ling smiled and tittered, and whispered bits of prayer as we moved through the darkness. "*Brigid, You have been so kind as to come to our aid with many remedies in the various sicknesses,*" she breathed as we climbed the stairs. The calico cat was waiting at the top, its golden eyes glaring balefully at me as it waited for its primary heat provider. "*Kindly hear our prayers and pour Your holy blessing from heaven upon this medicine.*"

"I think she heard you," I said as I staggered and hit the wall. "That's some powerful stuff you guys gave me.

"*That he who partakes of it,*" Meil-ling said through a giggle, "*may merit to receive health of both mind and body.*"

I landed in my bed and said nothing as Mei-ling carefully stripped me down to my long underwear and wrapped me in heavy blankets. She then dropped to her knees, placed her hands together in prayer and closed her single eye. "*Watch, dear Brigid, with those who wake or watch or weep tonight, and give your angels charge over those who sleep. Tend your sick ones, O Brigid, rest your weary ones, bless your dying ones, soothe your suffering ones, shield your joyous ones, and all for your love's sake. Amen."*

Well, as drugged as I was, there was something a little heart warming to have this delicate little nun praying over my soul, what little of it there may have been left after the heartbreak I'd given my parents. She rose to her feet, flashed me a smile as the cat took its rightful place on my feet, blew out the single candle, and bade me goodnight.

For a few moments I wrestled longer with my fading consciousness and why they had chosen Saint Brigid as their particular patron, and why they inserted her name to take precedence over both Jesus Christ and even God? Of course I could make no sense of it in my state though I'm sure I spent a good five befuddled minutes trying before giving up. As I allowed sleep to overcome me, I wondered what the new day and the predicated change of weather might portend. For some odd reason, I suspected it would be yet another event to make the institutional 'We regret to inform you of your son's death...' letter writers flex their typing fingers.

I was not to be disappointed.

Part Six
Dealers of Death

"Lad," the deep voice remarked in the darkness, "I haed thought I would need tae find some burial silver tae send tae yer mither. Just as well I didnae."

The effects of the laudanum made me thick headed and dozy and it took me several moments to pierce through the cobwebs that wrapped and held my mind to face the man behind the voice.

"I figured ye'd gone a corbie and mort kist when I heard the news. The Cardinal, bless her toes, told me different a few hours later."

I opened my eyes to the single candle flickering on my table. Illuminated like a cave bear by a campfire sat MacShaka, his normally dour facade, the one reminiscent of a freshly nutted bull chewing on a hornet, had softened somewhat. For a passing moment I wondered if he were both worried about me and happy to see me at the same time. He quickly put that thought to rest.

"The idea o' having tae replace two o' ye when recruiting is down tae the long in the horn or the wee cuddies is a thought I didnae want tae think about." He was being facetious of course, though not overly. A small smile flitted across his thick lips. Nearly a minute of silence passed, and then he said, "The Cardinal tells me you've been hard on yerself over Lukianos; dinnae be. He made his decision. Ye're no' a coward, Sikunder. Ye came ashore in the Coloe Vallis and ye ran in wi' Fremantle Freya." He sighed. "Ye may no' be Fionn himself, leading his Fianna, but ye're a right warrior when ye need it."

MacShaka's presence was surprising, but only just. I had suspected he would come to get me and the weather was supposed to break briefly, but still, there was something entirely satisfying to my battered soul that moment to have that affable mammoth sitting beside me chattering as I shed the final bonds of unconsciousness. When I was fully awake, MacShaka reached into his pack and pulled out a thermos.

"Sit up, ye mawkit limmer and enough wi' the dowie face." He unscrewed the lid and poured me a generous mug of piping hot coffee. "I ken fer a fact that the Cardinal can be some soor faced over the idea o' coffee, sae keep this tae yerself."

Well, I'd rarely been given a better gift in my life than the mug of coffee that morning. We sat in shivering silence while I sipped the powerful brew, and as my mind cleared, I allowed myself to boldly look upon the tartan monster and ask him questions.

"*Huzūra*, please, tell me what happed after the attack."

MacShaka pursed his lips for a moment and nodded, "Aye." He poured himself a coffee in a spare dirty mug he pulled from his pack and then sat back causing the chair to creak under his weight. "Old Talib Singh called it in, bless his soul. I'll miss that auld yin. It was all over the castrum in minutes and I had a call from the Warden tae investigate – he haein nae mair constables by the Ceallach. We lost contact quickly, but I wasnae worried really. Talib Singh was a tough auld chiel wi' years of fightin' on the frontier. If anyone would gie the Gliesiuns short shift and send them packin' it was him. Add tae that, he haed 50 rifles, plus you and Lukianos – that's a lot o' firepower in the valley, lad. Ol' Bonham wasnae worried either. He said he'd come up after the supper hour tae hae Singh debrief him – that's how worried he was. We didnae tarry, mind," he added seeing my look of shock. "The Gliesiuns haed opened up on our column and we'd lost contact. It was enough fer me tae take out three decurias myself in case Singh haed gaetten himself intae a tight spot." He glanced at me and toyed with the braids of his beard. "I'll admit, lad, that as time passed and we rode deeper intae the gleann and we couldnae raise anyone on the communications net, I daed begin tae worry a wee bit."

MacShaka paused to drink his coffee and stuff tobacco into his short wooden pipe. "I hae nae doubt that the Cardinal and all her hens wi' no' like my pipe, but that's too damned bad." Moments later he was puffing like a steam engine as he crossed his arms and looked at the cat curled up at my feet.

"We came upon them about six hours after they called it in. The weather slowed us down, and as time passed and we couldnae contact anyone, we became mair cautious. We found the remains of Talib and his column spread over about 100 meters or sae. Found every last one o' them save fer you. It was Sittina that found poor Lukianos, and a hard time she haed o' that. Young Jindan was beside herself wi' rage and was keenin' by the bank and ready tae take on the whole o' the Gliesiuns by herself. It was near dark then, when a party o' the nuns came down and explained they had ye up in the convent and that the Big Yin herself would no' let ye be moved. We decided tae head back soonest and come for ye later. Ye'd be safe, nae fear o' that. Sae here we are."

Well, that explained the events of the day, but my curiosity was piqued concerning the happenings since then. I wanted Coulthard to be terribly wrong about the indifference of the world to the death of Lukianos and so many others.

I was to be sorely disappointed.

"Poor Bohman was fit tae be tied. Was ready to take the rest o' his constables and race intae the valley and kill whatever he found. I managed tae talk some sense intae him, the crabbit footer, but I'm no' sure how much longer it'll last. I reported it up the chain – tae the centuria bimbashi and all the way tae the amir hisself. Duly noted was what I got in return. Said he'd, 'send a report in the next data packet tae Earth and dinnae lose anymair'."

"Oh my God," I replied in shock. Could they be so callous? Did the lives of those who died mean so very little? I was furious and terribly hurt at the same time. It was a very unfortunate reality I had to face. I meant nothing to the Legion in general and not much to my decuria in particular.

"I came up wi' Bohman, a half dozen o' his constables and two contubernium this morning, tae pick ye up and show the flag. Och," he grunted, "it'll be a miserable day wi' 70 centimetres o' snow tae head back down; supposed tae start snowing again this afternoon."

".Am I coming back?" I asked. MacShaka nodded.

".Aye, ye should be able tae ride a camel. We'll get ye back and hae the sawbones look on ye. This isnae done yet and I'll need all o' my jawans fit."

"Why did they do it?" I blurted. It was a rare day when the Tartan Hyperion was so chatty and I was bound and determined to make the best of it.

"Isnae that the question, now?" he replied as he tapped out his pipe on the chair arm and stamped out the embers. "Time tae gaet up and gae, lad; I'll wait fer ye in the common room."

Ten minutes later I found him and Coulthard talking before the fire – an amiable couple I supposed dryly as the dwarfish missus looked upon the bearded Colossus – each an unwinking gorgon engaging in small chat.

"Sikunder," MacShaka barked as I tooled into the room, "gaet yer gear." Coulthard had a number of nuns in the room with her; a pair of them was tacitly holding her back as she engaged with the behemoth of Panthera Centuria. "Cardinal," he boomed with a mock bow, "'tis a pleasure tae hae made yer acquaintance."

Several of the nuns looked down their nose at MacShaka, lips tight in disapproval at the use of such an insulting moniker. I took the opportunity to offer my own thanks, for they had saved my life.

"We are here to heal when healing is needed, Sikunder," she snapped rather severely. Clearly MacShaka had put her off for some reason. "*Brigid will protect you and preserve your life*," she added as she crossed herself. "*She will bless you in the land and not surrender you to the desire of her foes. Brigid will sustain you on your sickbed and restore you from your bed of illness.*" She spared MacShaka a glance. "Always a pleasure to meet a new Company employee, subedar."

"A tongue that would clip clouts," MacShaka growled as he led us out the door and into the cold and snow of the morning. The sky was a deep iron grey of low cloud, but the snow had tapered to light flurries giving the nuns a chance to keep the courtyard mostly clear.

"Wait for a moment, please, *Huzūra*," I asked as I gazed upon the monumental statue of Brigid and the four hooded nuns swinging their censers. The statue seemed to glare balefully, like a kind hearted judge about to sentence an errant lad. I'm not sure what drew me to it; that crudely carved face, those ingenuous eyes or the strongly gripped sword. Perhaps it was the Delphic suggestion of kindness and strength; in a world darkened by evil and death; a beacon of hope might exist in the wilderness where anyone could find compassion. It brought a tear to my eye, for in my six months here, I had seen little kindness that didn't come at a price. Not here though; here it was offered freely and gladly.

I found myself ascending the stairs to the deck, past the torches and the four nuns until I stood before the image of Brigid. That statue, nearly five meters tall; a narrow, wonderfully odd, almost abstract expressionism of pagan love and anger. It was a relic of old world – well, old, old word here on Samsāra – compassion and mercilessness. What was most odd was how I felt so drawn to those eyes. It was if they followed me, even as I stood upon that deck, and then sank slowly to my knees. Rarely had I gone to church as a child, and only with Nana Armstrong who spent more time elbowing me or flipping pages in the song book with a licked thumb and a vexatious eye. Why I felt so compelled now, I did not understand. Maybe I was just plain thankful to be alive.

"Sikunder," Mei-ling said as she knelt beside me. "Be safe in your travels." She brought her tiny hands in prayer and I found myself following suite. "*O Brigid, who hast commissioned Thy angels to guide and protect us, command them to be our assiduous companions from our setting out until our return; to clothe us with their invisible protection; to keep from us all evil, and especially from sin, to guide us to our heavenly home. Amen.*"

"Come on, lad," MacShaka demanded, though none too severely. As much as his lapsed Presbyterian soul must have been horrified with the heresy he was witnessing, he was also respectful, not so much at the convent and its nuns, but at my spiritual gratitude to whomsoever had saved my sorry life.

Outside the gate waited Sittina, Jindan, and Usman, the latter two nearly bowling me over in their embrace and eliciting a howl of pain from me and my fractured ribs. The rest, I was told, were waiting at the bottom of the three kilometre long trail.

"Help me baob!" MacShaka snapped as he grabbed Usman by the collar and tossed him onto the ground. "You!" he said as he shook his finger at Jindan, "you should know better. Tae stand there playin' the glaiket biddie; shame on ye, lass."

Jindan was fully embarrassed though she did glance at me slantendicular and flash a smile as she wiped away her tears.

MacShaka hoisted Usman by the scruff and gave him a good shake to remove the powdery snow. "And you, ye daft cuddy, are ye done wi' yer capers? Grab the lad's kit and make yerself useful, ye hither and yon bampot!"

Usman, untroubled at the dressing down, also smiled, took my pack and patted me lightly on the back. MacShaka flashed a cool glance at the nuns now standing idle in the exit of the convent while I waved at Mei-ling who offered a small wave back. As we walked away from the open gates towards Muneer and Makemba standing by a number of camels, I heard the crack of a stick to my right. I glanced over and halted in my tracks. I thought my heart would explode, and my breath came in gasps as if I was choking. I took a step backwards, fumbled for the pistol in my empty holster, and then patted my empty sash; nothing.

From the deep darkness of the forest a Gliesiun emerged an *Athand'u* warrior, well painted with a scarlet head, and well armed with a long barrelled pulse rifle in one hand and a *lancea* staff in the other. MacShaka saw the creature as well, and they drew on each other with a frightening rapidity that I thought would start a firefight right there.

"Stop!" shrieked Coulthard as she strode from the gate with a dozen of her well armed nuns at her back. "You will not raise your weapons on this hallowed ground!" She pointed at the Gliesiun. "*Subsisto!*"

Over a score of *Athand'u* warriors materialized from the shadows and every jawan but me had them in their rifle sights. The *Athand'u* returned the favour – aiming their pieces on us and hissing malevolently as they crouched low to attack.

I thought I would wet myself.

"Cardinal," MacShaka shouted as he eased his Khyber knife from his belt while he kept his pistol aimed at the lead warrior. "Care tae explain yerself?"

"No," Coulthard replied tersely, "I do not, nor can I since I didn't know they were coming."

"Are these the ones that massacred our lads?" MacShaka asked as he bared his teeth. The lead Gliesiun did the same, hissing louder, and spreading its powerful hind legs a little wider while raising its long tail for balance.

It was ready to strike.

"I don't know," Coulthard replied. She made a gesture, and her nuns split into two lines between us and the *Athand'u*. One line faced the Gliesiuns, the other ourselves. Both lines raised their rifles.

"Proper fuckin' firin' squad ye hae there, Cardinal," MacShaka jeered as he moved his pistol to aim it at the face of the closest cold-eyed nun.

"I think we can all lower our weapons," Coulthard hissed with an icy calm that was a polar opposite to my panic. She looked upon the lead Gliesiun. "*Proinde armis! Hodie!*" The Gliesiuns paused for a few moments before they lowered their weapons.

"Aye," MacShaka declared after a few moments, "I suppose we can." He slid his pistol into its holster and the Khyber knife into his sash. He glanced at me and then Coulthard. "I think it's time we all haed a wee chat. Is the tea on, lass?"

* * * * *

The common room was crowded, the packed bodies warming it to the point that I could shed my *postin, chapan,* and *sherwani* and sit there only in my *kurta* and *salwars*. MacShaka took a chair beside me, as did Sittina opposite. Usman and Jindan were banished to stand amongst the mass of whispering nuns waiting against the walls. Another figure entered, and I felt a thrill as I recognized Warden Bohman, black Stetson heavy with snow as he shrugged off his *chapan* coat to reveal the tarnished silver star pinned to his *sherwani*. He must have been close to Pacatus, for we'd been waiting for only about 10 minutes or so. His cold flinty eyes fell on the *Athand'u* chief who squatted beside Coulthard. His hand moved to his pistol.

"Not here, Warden," Coulthard warned as she stood and focused her piercing dark eyes on Bohman. The Gliesiun, sensing the danger, rose slowly, her hand resting on a boomerang shaped throwing knife called a *yoongz*. Coulthard raised her hand at the creature. "*Pausa*," she said. The creature lowered itself back to a squat, though it didn't take its eyes off of Bohman.

Bohman pointed at the Gliesiun as he walked past me. "That bitch makes a hornet look cuddly." As quaint as the words were, I could hear real rage in his voice. It was taking every effort for him not to draw and kill that Gliesiun right then and there. He took a seat beside MacShaka, his hand never leaving his pistol. "Should be damned to all this and turn that bitch into buzzard's bait."

"Aye," MacShaka mused, "that lichtsome scunner would be better two meters down."

"Jesus, the pair of you," Sittina snapped in a rare show of annoyance. "Enough already with the down home wit." I nodded with a passing smile and received enough of an elbow in my fractured ribs from MacShaka to know, in an explosion of pain, that I'd crossed the line.

A silence ensued – a deadly earnest cloud of rage only kept in check by Coulthard and her nuns at our back. The Gliesiun was here alone; a war chief with no fear before the humans and ready to die in a heartbeat if that's what it took. I wondered if we could possibly accomplish anything before the knives and pistols were drawn.

"*Peace I leave with you,*" Coulthard said to break the silence as she crossed herself, "*my peace I give unto you: not as the world giveth, give I unto you. Let not your heart be troubled, neither let it be afraid.*"

"Well, now that we got that outghta the way," Bohman said as he pulled out his pipe and a bag of tobacco, "let's get to the point and find out from this here bitch born sorry, just why it was she and her kin decided to kill off 20 of my constables." He never raised his voice, and his words were delivered in that down home matter-of-fact affability that would have brought a smile to my lips had it not been for his eyes. They were the eyes of a killer.

"Her name is Bellona Maia," Coulthard began as a nun brought in a tea pot and several cups, "and she is the war chief of the *Ustawo* clan of the *Athand'u.*"

"Ye named yer pet?" MacShaka asked with some surprise. "Very nice, Cardinal."

"If you would prefer, subedar," Coulthard delivered with an iciness that cooled me to the heart, "we can dispense with any pretence of trying to stop a massacre and begin it all this very moment. You can certainly kill her now, and then the warriors she has hiding in the trees can fall upon your jawans and constables and it will all be finished in time for supper. Prefer that do you?" she asked in a voice gravelled by anger. MacShaka, in one of those rare moments, was bullied to silence.

"Her name is Bellona and she can speak through this," she said as she laid a compu-pad on a table and initiated a translation program. "Speak," she said to the Gliesiun.

"*Aoeheikh,*" the compu-pad said in Gliesiun after a few moments.

"Why did you kill the police?" Coulthard asked.

"*Hkikah - kai'aih eiailoso'?*" the compu-pad asked a few moments later.

The Gliesiun looked upon Coulthard for a moment, then back at Bohman. Those pale blue eyes, reptilian in their calculating coldness, never left him when she stated, "*Kai'aih awa'ahar- an t'han.*"

"*They came to kill us.*"

"Lot of nooses in your family tree," Bohman shot back. "Damned if'n they were there to do anything but ride out to Svarga and back."

Bellona quickly fired back a few words in Latin before she gave up to her mother tongue. "*Luk'nue alll-ouorfool'nue oung''gnedz uthd'an-lae ig'hguaro okn-olkhung.*"

"*They were coming to kill us. It was foretold. They had 50 rifles and they were coming to kill us. Woman and child, male and female.*"

"Who told you that pack of lies?" Bohman asked. "They had no orders for that because I gave 'em the damned orders! Svarga and back and spend the night if the weather turned nasty, and if that ain't a damned fact, well then God's a possum!"

Bellona suddenly looked perplexed, if a saurian horse-faced warrior painted red and armed to the teeth could look perplexed. MacShaka sighed and Coulthard cleared her throat and advised, "I doubt the Texan idioms translate well, Warden."

"Not my damned problem, Cardinal," he snapped as he pulled his pipe out of his mouth.

"Please don't smoke in here," Coulthard barked with the disapproving tones of a mother.

"Then I'll be a-takin' myself outside and not be a-comin' back, Mother Superior." He was angry and petulant, and as MacShaka pulled out his own pipe, Coulthard opted to give in.

The consequence of Bohman leaving was obvious; it would be a bloodbath.

"Warden," Coulthard reasoned after he'd lit up and puffed for a few moments on his pipe, "I believe you when you say that the column had no orders to attack the Gliesiuns, but clearly, someone told the *Athand'u* that this was the case."

"Mighta coulda been the *Chúsheng*, I s'pose," Bohman replied after a moment's thought. He glanced at me before adding, "They were mad enough to raise Hell and stick a chunk under it after those Legion jawans shot them up."

Bellona spoke a few words. "*Not the animals*," the compu-pad translated. She looked at Bohman and MacShaka.

"*Et'moru.*"

"Awa wi' ye," MacShaka hissed as he leaned forward, "what the fuck daed she just say?"

Bohman was equally wide-eyed. "She's all hat and no cattle. No way that's true."

"Aye," MacShaka growled with a nod. "Ham-a-haddie that is. Utter bollocks."

It meant nothing to me though clearly I was in the minority. The nuns whispered fearfully amongst themselves, and MacShaka and Bohman, though unconvinced at whatever the Gliesiun had said, looked grim. I leaned over and whispered to Sittina, "What the hell is the *Et'moru*?"

"They are a Gliesiun tribe, jawan," Coulthard said as she tented her fingers and placed her forehead on them. "They were given land down in the Cebrenia Vallis, far to the south and away from humans and other Gliesiuns and that is where they should be."

"Fucking torn faced crabbit murderous animals," MacShaka exclaimed through clenched teeth. "Worst fucking decision the UN ever made was bringing that tribe o' killers tae this colony."

I'd never heard of them, but clearly they were an obscure yet decidedly deadly threat. Bohman pointed the stem of his pipe at Bellona. "You tryin' to tell me that some *Et'moru* told you and your beef-headed crew that the police were there to kill ye, and you might had better kill 'em first?" He sat back disgusted. "That's so God damned crooked that if'n ye swallowed a nail, ye'd spit up a corkscrew."

Bellona looked on in confusion, blinking and then looking at Coulthard.

"Warden," Coulthard sighed.

"No!" Bohman exploded, his hand once again moving to his pistol. "She's more slippery than a pocket full of pudding with her lies. *Et'moru* up here in the valley, and no one knowing about it? That's bullpuckey if'n I ever heard of it."

"Aye, she's gien us nae end o' havers wi' that story," MacShaka grunted.

Bohman tamped more tobacco into his pipe and then waved it about in anger. "Christ sakes, Calamity Jane," he groused, "a God damned guilty fox hunts his own holes, here. That's the damndest story to make up for those capers!" He suddenly stood up, his moustache bristling in rage. "I'll be damned if'n I listen to that anymore. You," he glared at Bellona who returned his gaze defiantly, "I'll be back here with a column big enough to make a hornet's nest look cuddly. You'd better dig in somewhere because I'll root you out faster than a prairie fire with a tail wind!"

"Tyrel," MacShaka growled, "take a seat fer a few mair minutes." He turned his attention to Coulthard. "How long hae they been here, the *Athand'u*?"

"Years," Coulthard replied as she picked up her cup of tea. "This particular clan has been here at least three years. They work summers on the road being built from Ophir and then winter in the valley. Why?"

"Yeah," Bohman demanded as he eyed Bellona. "Why?"

For several moments MacShaka gazed upon the Gliesiun, his dark eyes focused intently as he mused over her story. "Tyrel, it's damned likely," he murmured, "that story's no' worth a tinker's curse. But damn it, it's the strangest but most logical tale tae come up wi' tae explain what they daed."

"They rubbed out my column, Angus," Bohman replied with a savage glint. "I don't really care who was a-tellin' them to do it!"

"I sure as hell dae," MacShaka scolded. "I sure as hell care if there's a group o' *Et'moru* around here." He looked at Bohman. "Dinnae you?"

That seemed to have him at a loss, and silence ensued.

"How would they get up here if they are so far south?" I asked. It was one of those moments, not as rare as I would have liked, that I spoke up without really thinking.

All eyes suddenly focused on me, including Bellona, which was a truly frightening moment.

"Aye, weel, that's the damned question now isnae it, ye wee horn idle bauchle," MacShaka replied without much of his usual rancour.

"That boy could talk the legs off'n a chair," Bohman remarked with the hint of a smile. He looked at Coulthard. "Well, nanny, you been here longest, any ideas how the *Et'moru* could sneak their way into this valley?"

"There are plenty of ways," Coulthard replied as she massaged her temples. "The easiest would be from the east, through Gehon Vallis, Tractus Vallis or Amenthes Vallis. They all feed into Gleann Ceallach from the east." She raised her head to look at MacShaka and Bohman. "No one watches the valles and no one is watching the *Et'moru*. They live 200 kilometres south as the crow flies – double that to enter this gleann as secretly as they have, if they have."

"Aye, and why would they come here?" MacShaka asked. He looked at Bellona and leaned towards her. "You, ye daft biddie, you answer that now." He spoke slowly and deliberately towards the compu-pad. "Why are the *Et'moru* here?"

Bellona did not answer for a moment. Then deigning to ignore MacShaka's insolence, she replied simply, "*Ahkhoeng.*"

"*War,*" the compu-pad said.

"Och, that dinnae makes sense," MacShaka replied though with far less enthusiasm.

"Doesn't it though?" Coulthard asked.

"Nae," MacShaka retorted, "it disna make any fucking sense. Tae coorie down in the damned gleann, proddin' and threatenin' the daft puddin' headed *Athand'u* tae pick a fight wi' the Legion and the Constabulary? They damn weel ken they'll gaet a right sherrack when we roll in wi' a hundred rifles and a *barra* head o' steam. I dinnae buy it for a moment."

This, however, was not true, for he was losing enthusiasm for his argument as fast as he made it. Coulthard said nothing as she looked into the flames while Bohman merely puffed on his pipe and looked sour. Silence overcame us for a few moments until the Gliesiun slowly rose from her position. She grunted a sentence and moved towards the door.

"*My family is here and we will stay for now.*"

Coulthard nodded and Bohman was nearly apoplectic as he stood. "You're one bubble off plumb, if'n ye're gonna let that mad bitch and her brood unhitch their wagon here."

"Warden," Coulthard replied with icy resolve, "what I do in my convent is my business, not yours."

"Your convent falls under UN law, missy," Bohman shot back.

"And your constables enter this vallis only by my sufferance," Coulthard replied with a thin smile and the slightest movement of her hand. There was a rustle, and suddenly a dozen pulse rifles appeared amongst the shadowy nuns.

"You and yer holy harridans are as crazy as bullbats," Bohman roared as he stormed past Bellona and out the door.

The *palaver* was over and Coulthard and her nuns moved off to the chapel while Sittina led Usman and Jindan out into the courtyard. MacShaka was as still as a stone idol as he looked into the flames – a musing Yeti with the weight of the world on his shoulders. I wasn't sure what was running through that cunning mind of his, for I'd understood, I mean really understood, little of the issues facing us. What I did understand was that 51 men and women, including my comrade Lukianos, had been killed by the *Athand'u* who in turn had been put up to it by a shadowy and horrific clan of Gliesiuns from far to the south called the *Et'moru*. That explanation had been met by hot-headed derision that had cooled to fear at the possibility that there could be truth in it. That part I understood; it was the loathing and terror of this clan that I did not. What made them, I wondered, any worse than the most bloodthirsty of the *Chúsheng*, the most malicious of the Black Hand, or the cruellest of MacGrogan-Singh's Fearadadh Boys? The reactions seemed to be bordering on hysteria, and unable to contain myself, I said as much to MacShaka.

"Hysteria, lad?" he said with an alarming calmness that took me aback. "Aye, I suppose it is." There was a long pause that made

me distinctly uncomfortable and then MacShaka droned in a deep
bass,

> *"Wi' sword and wi' dagger*
> *They rushed on him rude;*
> *The twa gallant Gordons*
> *Lie bathed in their blude.*
> *Frae the sprigs o' the Dee*
> *To the mouth o' the Tay,*
> *The Gordons mourn for him,*
> And curse Inveraye."

"Uh, I don't follow, *Huzūra.*"

"The killings, Sikunder," MacShaka said as he slowly tamped
tobacco into his pipe. "Soon enough we wi' hae killings on our
heid."

I was at a loss, for the man had sunk into some kind of
profound Celtic reverie. For several moments, he puffed on his
pipe in silence, and when he spoke it was in another deep
monotone dirge.

"When I was a havildar, twelve years ago on Gliesium, the
Panthera Centuria was assigned to the Hellas sector; a handfu' o'
valleys in the northeast, close tae the dark side o' the planet."

It took me a moment to recall that Gliesium was a tidally
frozen planet with one half in perpetual daylight and the other in
deep frozen darkness. The habitable zone that lay between the icy
darkness and broiling daylight was the domain of the Gliesiuns
and their civil war.

"We were paired wi' 3,000 or sae *Ech'cha* and given the
miserable task o' haulding the Warendo Vallis; a cold barren land
o' rock and ice; a terrible place tae lie up for weeks on end, livin' in
our wee tents and on hard rations, and freezin' our asses off.
There wasnae fightin'; we just sat around in the cauld waitin' for

the day when warriors o' the *Ll'oughlsong* tribe would arrive and we would hae tae hauld out against them. We knew they were comin', mind," MacShaka added with a sigh. "They'd been makin' their way north taewards us, burnin' an' killin'. We waited, dug in, and froze until the day when they arrived; a column o' 20,000 warriors and their followers if there was one. We haed a strong position, but no' much support; nae artillery, nae air support, an' only modest orbital support. They attacked, and by the end o' the fairst day, half o' our numbers were gone. Nearly half o' the *Ll'oughlsong* were dead or wounded foreby, and we were in terrible shape. We couldnae hauld them off if they came at us again, but we were preparin' tae make a final stand fer we could never outrun the bastards. Never," he repeated.

"Weel," he said after a long pause, "in the night, we haed a visitor – one o' the *Et'moru*. She told us there were several hundred nearby, and we negotiated for their help. Weapons, ammunition, equipment, and they would provide us assistance in the comin' fight. The HQ bought the deal, and an hour later, about 1,000 of the *Et'moru* fell upon the surviving *Ll'oughlsong* and killed them."

"All of them?" I asked in surprise. "All 10,000 or so?"

MacShaka nodded, "Aye. All o' them. The *Et'moru* had been poorly armed, nothin' but their blades, some pulse rifles we gave them, and their hate. The next mornin' there was no' a thing tae see save for a few hundred *Et'moru*, dripping blood from their heids tae their tails." He looked at me with haunted eyes and I felt a chill go through me. "I've no' ever seen the like, lad. No' ever in my life. They didnae stop at killing them, Sikunder, they completely destroyed them. They ripped them tae pieces, skinned them, spread them about like a great crimson carpet. They even ate the young that accompanied the tribe – scores o' the wee bairns."

I felt my blood run cold and I shivered.

"The noise they made, Sikunder, as the *Et'moru* killed them in the night. Help me boab if I ever again hear the like." He paused and seemed to be searching for words as his lips moved and no sound came out. "How dae ye describe it? The shriekin' and the screamin' at the top o' their lungs in an agony I couldnae ever imagine. The *Et'moru* destroyed them as slowly and as painfully as they could. In the mornin' under the light of their sun, amongst sae much gore, the *Et'moru* were at their merriest. Playin' wi' the heids o' the bairns like toys. Lad, the day those sounds and sights leave me will be the day I die." He paused as he cupped his face in his huge hands. When he looked at me, I could have sworn he had a tear in his eye. "That mornin', Sikunder, I didnae think I could die fast enough."

Well, I'd imagined I'd hear many things from the Scotch gorilla, but that horrifying account of the Warendo Vallis and the look of horror that still haunted a giant of a man, whom I looked up to as more of a monster than human, was not one of them. It left me sick and mortally terrified. My God, I thought as I clasped my shaking hands, if it terrified MacShaka, what should it do to me? To be honest, it didn't do much at the time but elicit the normal vapours I had whenever danger presented itself. I was simply ignorant of the truth and I lacked the imagination to visualize what the creatures were capable of.

We both sat in silence for a while until MacShaka seemed to shake himself from his trance. He tapped out the tobacco of his pipe and stood. "Come on, lad," he growled, "I suspect we'll hae a hot day or two comin'."

I wasn't sure what he meant by that, but as we exited into the icy courtyard to see the score of Gliesiuns hunkered down under tarps, and the gates closed and barred with a handful of armed nuns in the windows, it suddenly occurred to me that the convent was taking on a distinctly Alamo feeling.

MacShaka led us through the main gate and out into the snowy field before the convent. There Bohman was waiting with some of his constables along with Sittina and the rest of my contubernium. MacShaka paused as he looked upon them. The other contubernium was on the trail, and as the snow fell heavier, piling up around us even as he mused on his course of action, he finally said, "I think it'll be too late tae get back tae the castrum today. Snow is comin' down fast as weel. Perhaps we should gather our keelies and spend the night in the convent here and see what the mornin' brings."

Sittina seemed as surprised as I was, and Bohman looked stunned. He was quick to speak up. "If'n you're a-thinkin' what I think ye're a-thinkin', Angus, ye don't hang yer wash on someone else's line."

MacShaka arched an eyebrow. "If that *Athand'u* quean is nae haverin', then it may be worth our while tae stay around a wee bit."

"If'n what she is a-sayin' is the truth," Bohman retorted, "an' I think she's on a first name basis with the bottom of the deck, then it'd be better for us to high-tail it back to the castrum and rethink life."

"And leave them?" Sittina observed. "Not only them," she said as she indicated the convent, "but what about the settlements? What about Svarga? If there are indeed *Et'moru* in the valley, then is it not our duty to stay and defend the settlers?"

"Defend them?" Bohman replied in surprise. He tipped his Stetson back. "Lady, what do think ye're going to defend them with? I'll say yer jawans are brave enough to shoot craps with the Devil himself, but we don't have numbers. I have a half dozen constables and you have some 20 jawans. What are ye a-thinkin' ye're goin' to be a-doin' with that?"

"Waitin' the night at least," MacShaka repeated. "Havilder, get Cong up here with his contubernium while I gae and chat wi' the Grannie Mutchie o' the place."

MacShaka turned and headed into the convent leaving me to huddle with my contubernium. Muneer gave me a frosty nod which was as near a hug as I would ever get from the mad mullah, while Makemba, Yee, and Fung greeted me with rare warmth, touching my sleeve and sparing me little smiles. Jindan held my hand and Usman grinned with boyish excitement at the thought of a coming fight – it was a fine reunion of sorts. Bohman and his constables stood idle, looking peevish at the thought of having to stay, until Bohman finally stumped over, cut me out like a calf from the herd, and placed a skeletal hand on my shoulder.

"Haven't had the chance to say, hoss, that seein' ye alive and breathin' had me wantin' to throw my hat over the windmill. When word came down, it crossed my mind that you might coulda been dead. Well, I felt so low I couldn't have jumped off'n a dime then. Glad to see you here; might need that pulse rifle of yours."

It was infinitely pleasing that the old Texas Ranger was happy to see me. I smiled and basked in his rough affection, even when he added with a wink, "Any mule's tail can catch cockleburs though."

Moments later MacShaka came back out and indicated with his thumb that we ought to go inside. "Och, she's no' happy about it," he said with a grim smile, "but she at least sees the logic. If there are *Et'moru* about, then the Cardinal and her shower o' carpin' tawpies might be a target, and the extra help will be useful tae her."

We made to move inside, but MacShaka placed a hand on my shoulder. "No' you, lad, you and the Warden are comin' wi' me for a wee ride."

I protested, though not loudly, of my fractured ribs and MacShaka spared me a wintry glance. "Michty me," he grunted. "Sair ribs are no' enough tae be on the panel, ye dilly daw. Get yer gear. We'll gae below tae the Ceallach and see the lay o' the land." He looked behind him as the Gliesiun named Bellona exited the convent with a half dozen of her warriors in tow. "Aye, here comes that carnaptious Bessie tae gie us a haund."

"You keep yer saddle oiled and yer gun greased with that one," Bohman groused as he mounted his horse.

Minutes later, Bellona and her warriors were leading us back down the three kilometre trail towards the river Ceallach. It was unnerving really, the silence beneath the low cloud and the falling snow, the piercing cold and the knowledge that there might be any number of the most murderous animals in creation watching us. The path itself increased my apprehension, for it was a narrow, meandering trail only a few meters wide beside the Artus Flumen, now nearly frozen over in ice. We could ride side by side between the river and the looming forest on our right but just barely and my gaze was constantly drawn to that cheerless darkness within the trees and its foreboding threat. About 20 minutes in, we moved to the side of the trail to allow Havilder Cong Fu-chi and his contubernium to come through. He paused as his jawans moved on, and while he looked upon the *Athand'u* with fury, MacShaka grilled him on whether he'd seen anything.

Cong shook his head. "Very quiet down there, as it should be in this weather. The trail is thick with snow and everyone is sitting in their homes and before a fire while we wander around in the cold."

"*Shù dǎo húsūn sàn*," MacShaka muttered as he looked up at the falling snow. I glanced at Cong who smiled and said, "When the tree falls, the monkeys scatter."

It was a rare day when I could follow the idiomatic musings of the disparate jawans of the Legion, and MacShaka as he weaved amongst Glaswegian, Gaelic, and Chinese was perhaps the worst.

"*Hěn gāoxìng jiàn dào nǐ*, jawan," Cong said as he sat plump and smiling on his camel. "Good to see you," he offered as I looked confused.

As he rode off, for a moment I felt less of a stranger in their midst than I ever had before; a small sign of acceptance perhaps, or maybe just mere good manners. I wasn't sure in the end, but that bit of welcome brought a smile to my face. MacShaka did what he could to erase it.

"Come, lad, ye spurtle-leggit bampot. Shift yer arse."

We continued on and the silence again encroached. Only the softest sound of falling snowflakes could be heard over the faint jingle of the horse and tundra camel bridles. My anxiety, already aroused, rose to new heights as we approached the river Ceallach; for again I felt the fear that we were being watched. My disquiet grew over the remaining minutes it took us to make our way down to the Ceallach, for memories of that horrific battle and my subsequent cowardly flight were rolling over me in waves of piercing guilt. MacShaka noted my silence and decided to ride beside me.

"Lad," he said softly, "ye hae a face like a half shut knife. Stop wi' the dour misery and keep yer wits about ye."

I said nothing as I fought my emotions, the terrible guilt gnawing at my soul as we approached the scene of my cowardice. When we passed the deadfalls over the Artus where I'd hidden and nearly frozen to death, it took everything not to start weeping right there. When, several minutes later, we were at the site of the massacre itself, with the litter of frozen horses and tundra camels protruding obscenely from 70 centimetres of fallen snow, and the many less intrusive humps that marked the dead constables and deputies, I lost my composure and tears rolled down my cheeks. I looked at the snowy mound of my fallen tundra camel, Gomeda, and knew that Lukianos was likely buried in the drifts surrounding it and his own tundra camel. I wanted to *koosh* my beast right then and go over to that spot, but MacShaka eyed me for a moment and shook his head.

"Let it gae, lad," was all he said as he reached over to pat my hand. "I brought ye here for that very reason. Let it gae."

Get back on the horse; I should have known that was why he brought me.

"Ye know," Bohman said as he shivered in the cold wind that was blowing down the vallis and then removed his Stetson to flick off the piling snow, "if'n it's true and there are some of them *Et'moru* darkenin' the valley, then we're a few pickles short of a barrel to be a-sittin' here and a-jawin' about what to do with ourselves."

"Aye," MacShaka said with a nod, "but I need tae see the lay o' the land."

"The lay of the land?" Bohman replied as he shuddered beneath his *chapan*. He looked southeast towards the castrum. "The lay of the land says we're 15 kilometres away from safety in the middle of a winter storm with a yard of snow on the ground and the rumour that we might could have a horde of *Et'moru* around our ears if'n we aren't careful." He spat, wiped the snow and ice from his walrus moustache, and flashed a grin. "Cold as my ex-wife's heart out here and we're a-sittin' around arguin' with a wooden Indian.

That brought a grin to MacShaka's face for a moment before he nudged his tundra camel towards the Gliesiun named Bellona. He reached into his *chapan* and pulled out a compu-pad. "Bellona," he said as he switched it to Gliesiun, "where are the rest of your kin?"

Bellona said nothing as she scanned the field. Visibility was low as the heavy snow fell – no more than 50 meters or so. She looked east, towards the invisible tree line, and finally rumbled something that was translated to, "I do not know."

"Aye, that's nae help," MacShaka snapped.

I looked upon the distant tree line myself, visible by using my tactical contact lenses, but saw nothing of interest save for the distant Cimmerian shade beneath the canopy. No movement or activity of any sort, and clearly this was a worry for Bellona. She again spoke, a longer croaking that was translated to, "They should be at the tree line. They were told to wait in the tree line with scouts watching the field to see us."

"There ain't no one there," Bohman said as he scanned the invisible tree line. "Guess we might had better go and look for these varmints," he added with his quaint Texan charm that sounded suspiciously hollow now. I noted a tinge of concern in his voice as he flicked the reins of his horse and began walking towards the western side of the valley.

"Aye, we might as well take a look," MacShaka agreed, with as much enthusiasm as he could muster. The Gliesiuns led the way, loping in the snow with a caution that had me reaching for my pulse rifle. Though both MacShaka and Bohman were still not convinced of the story of the *Et'moru*, both were showing enough reserve to have their weapons out and their eyes peeled.

What made the situation more alarming as we plodded through the snowstorm was not the fear of duplicity from the

Athand'u; no, it was the fear that as we closed the tree line a shrieking horde would emerge to slaughter us where we stood. Neither MacShaka nor Bohman showed concern any longer about the creatures walking amongst us. They now believed, if not firmly believed, that the real threat was that tribe of murderous animals that might be even now running loose in the gleann.

The tree line appeared, dim through the veil of falling snow, and still, no movement could be seen. As we closed the distance, our tundra camels plodding in 60 centimetres of snow while the Gliesiuns struggled through the drifts, the angst we were feeling increased. According to Bellona, her kin should have been in there – 100 or so adults and young waiting to know the outcome of her meeting with Coulthard. We saw nothing, however, as we approached the tree line itself and the shadows beyond. Bellona looked long into the murk, a near darkness in the low light and thick canopy. She muttered in her deep voice;

"*Gik irdungamkusa shuku.*"

"I see and hear nothing."

"Aye," MacShaka said as he *kooshed* his tundra camel. I did the same and hopped off with a grunt from my aching ribs and powered up my pulse rifle. I paused to power up my pistol and then slid it back into my holster.

Bohman slid off his horse and tied the reins to a fallen tree branch. "Dark as coffin air in here," he muttered as he pulled a pulse rifle out of a holster on his saddle. "I ain't a-goin' te lie," he added almost under his breath as he moved to stand beside MacShaka and myself, "makes me as nervous as a whore in church."

"Aye," MacShaka said as he stepped off to proceed deeper into the forest. "Keep yer wits about ye," he whispered. I fell in line behind him and heard Bohman a few steps behind me. The

143

Gliesiuns led the way, penetrating the deep gloom with their own pulse rifles at the ready. Even beneath the heavy canopy, there was snow, just to the top of my ankles, that made the going slow. We were tryin to be as quiet as possible, but the racket we made as we stepped on hidden sticks wouldn't have fooled a deaf man. We had been moving perhaps 10 minutes when the faintest of smells became apparent – an iron smell mixed with offal. It stopped me cold, for I'd smelled that noisome mixture months before in the trenches of the Coloe Vallis where scores of Black Hand had died, blasted to pieces by our recoilless rifles.

"Mind yourselves," MacShaka whispered as we stepped through the snow towards a massive round erratic – a lorry sized rock left behind from some long forgotten glacier. "Help me boab," MacShaka said as he stopped, for the horrific smell was much stronger. The rock sat on a low rise thick with trees, and as the Gliesians topped it they halted and simply stared. "Come," MacShaka whispered. I didn't want to for I knew what lay beyond. Reluctantly I found myself following, my legs guiding an unwilling mind to the rise and the sight beyond. When I finally topped it and leaned on the erratic, I felt my stomach heave, and despite the agony of my fracture ribs, I vomited with hopeless abandon. Laid out before us, in a shattered camp of tarps and blankets, lay the remains of the *Athand'u*. It was as MacShaka had described in his own experience years before on Gliesium. The *Athand'u* had been slaughtered, but it had not stopped at mere slaughter. Their appalling destruction had been an exercise in calculated butchery with bodies rendered so completely as to be unable to tell where one ended and one began. They had been turned into a literal carpet of horror with limbs, flesh, offal, and hides spread over the forest floor like a scarlet wash. Only the heads appeared to have been saved, for they hung like ghastly Christmas ornaments from the branches far above, or were placed on stakes punched into the ground, or hung on the trunks of the trees. The annihilation was so utterly complete as to make it impossible to decipher what had happened, and save for the heads, what these creatures might have been in life.

It was like witnessing a true and complete hatred; a contempt for life that was so absolute and exhaustive that to kill a *Athand'u* was not near enough – one had to obliterate it from existence with only the head remaining as a hint of what had been so completely destroyed.

I found myself vomiting again.

"Bear up, lad," MacShaka whispered. He quickly called the heinous scene in to both the castrum and the convent. He looked at Bellona and her crew who stood frozen in horror and rage. "Aye, doesnae this all make sense now," he said. "Och, it all makes sense."

Bohman was wide-eyed as he gazed upon the scene; he crouched low, his pulse rifle at the ready as he looked beyond, deeper into the forest. "There ain't nuthin' out there, Angus," he croaked in a voice thick with emotion, "but I don't know how long that'll last. Best we think about liftin' up stakes and headin' to that convent before it's too late."

MacShaka nodded. "Aye," he muttered as he punched me in the arm. "Come on, lad, sort yerself out."

I had my rifle at the ready as my side burned from my vomiting. MacShaka took a few steps forward and knelt beside Bellona.

"Time tae gae," he said into the compu-pad. The Gliesiuns didn't move; they just squatted there staring at the horror before them. "What guid will ye dae sittin' here waitin' fer them tae return and finish ye off," MacShaka growled. "Come along, they'll be at the convent soon enough. We'll hauld up there an' ye'll hae yer chance fer revenge then."

It was an agonizing minute as I fought down the rising panic, the same panic that had given me such speed to flee from Lukianos, while the Gliesiuns decided their fate. With no more emotion than a ships' wooden figurehead, Bellona and her warriors turned from that abominable scene to make their way back to the tree line. We hurried along behind them, throwing caution to the wind, for one fact of that slaughter stood out even to a rookie such as myself – the killings hadn't happened too long before.

"Might hae been an hour or two ago," MacShaka said as he mounted his tundra camel. "No mair, that's fer sure. Almost nae snow on the site and the smell still *barra* strong. Aye, we show caution now and some speed, for I dinnae wish tae race that shower o' murderers back up the Artus."

We moved quickly, following our tracks back through the thickening shroud of snow. When we reached the massacre site of the column, MacShaka raised his arm and we stopped. Bohman tipped his hat back and spat.

"Damn it," he muttered. "That's about as welcome as an outhouse breeze."

I glanced where he was looking and saw the double set of Gliesiun tracks – tracks not made by Bellona and her kin. "We sure as hell didn't need that."

"No," MacShaka said as he slapped the rump of his tundra camel with a switch.

"Tracks come from the north," Bohman reported as he squinted into the distance. "Two God damned hoots and a holler away to the north and the east. Come out of the tree line about a klick north of the slaughter."

"Aye," MacShaka sniffed. "And whaur daed they gae?"

Bohman was off his horse and knee deep in the snow. While the others looked on, he examined the tracks, and then pointed towards Artus Vallis. "Into the tree line there and movin' faster than a sneeze through a screen door; two of them by the looks of it." He looked at MacShaka. "Scouts, I'd say."

MacShaka nodded and glanced at Bellona. She and her Gliesiuns were motionless, their eyes focused on the shadows beneath the trees. Their stillness was unnerving – like watching pointer dogs on a scent. MacShaka said nothing as he too scanned the forest.

"We'd best be gaen," he said. "You," he barked to Bellona. "Tell yer pack of savages tae take the lead." He paused after Bellona's pale eyes fell on him. "*Kalamlu ki ikurgirluaash* or some such fucking thing." Bellona glared at him with owl eyes before grunting something to her warriors.

We moved out – cautious as we made our way back up the trail – but with more speed as no one was keen on meeting the *Et'moru*. It was well after lunch, and what with my vomiting and very little to eat for the last few days, I had to admit to being absolutely famished. As the Gliesiuns led us up the narrow track, and with MacShaka in front and Bohman behind, I rested my pulse rifle across my saddle and dug around for a stuff sack with food. I pulled out cold *naan* bread, in fact it was just shy of frozen in the -20 degree weather, but I didn't mind. I shoved it into my *sherwani* for 10 minutes and let my body heat thaw it. The trees were tall on either side, and although their canopy didn't completely obliterate the sky, it was enough to both darken the trail and keep much of the snow off; so much so that we made decent progress. It was when I began breaking off pieces of *naan* bread and thinking a decent meal at the end of this harrowing experience was something I could look forward to, that I was struck from the side.

I had no warning. As I popped a piece of the bread into my mouth, I heard a shriek – a shrill piercing cry as a body emerged from a pile of snowy brush to leap the meters towards me. I didn't even have the opportunity to look before a creature bowled into me and I was lying on my back in the snow with the most hideous of Gliesiuns lying atop me. It was *Et'moru*, small with its equine head painted in stripes of blue and black; large orange hate-filled eyes that seemed to glare blazing fury; a row of filed teeth that gnashed and ground in my face; and a body covered in a carapace of black and red stripes. It held a long narrow *pugio* dagger in one hand while the other grasped at my face with its three powerful fingers and squeezed. There was an explosion of pain as my skin ripped, and I suddenly tasted blood even as I began to suffocate beneath that grip. How it didn't kill me instantly with a thrust of that razor sharp *pugio* is beyond me, bad timing or poor aim, I don't know. But as it squeezed my face, I screamed and wailed and did what I could to defend myself – kicking, punching, wriggling, and wrestling to break its death grip. I heard other shrieks and cries, and as I felt my consciousness fade and heard that far too familiar roaring in my ears, there was a gunshot near my side and the *Et'moru* stiffened and fell on top of me, its head drooling gore on my face.

"Fuck sakes get it off!" I shrieked as I kicked my way from beneath its dead weight. I pawed blood from my face as MacShaka pulled me to my feet and shoved my pulse rifle into my hands.

"Jesus fucking Christ!" he roared as another *Et'moru* spun around in front of him with an *Athand'u* head in its hand. "Dinnae stand there and dae fuck all!"

I was stung to action, and before he could say another thing, I drew my pistol and was firing at the darting creature as a pair of *Athand'u* tackled it to the ground. The *Et'moru's* piercing hate-filled scream nearly made my ears bleed, and as the three struggled into a roiling Gliesiun heap, I holstered my pistol, dug in the snow for my dropped rifle, and mindlessly tapped a button on the side of my rifle, heard the 'snick' as the 30 centimetre serrated bayonet popped out. As the creature's head was momentarily pinned, I roared and thrust the blade into its neck. It nearly wrenched my rifle from my hands as it screamed and bucked, but the two *Athand'u* held it and I thrust again, burying the blade into the base of the creature's skull. Right then and there I felt a rage that had never struck me before – as if my many months of fear and anger, pent up within an acquiescent body were suddenly released. I bellowed at the top of my lungs and I stabbed and stabbed and stabbed until I could no longer see straight.

"Easy, lad," MacShaka's deep voice came from somewhere, and I felt powerful arms grab me. "Easy, lad," he said again.

The red of my tunnel vision drained away, leaving a grisly vision of the mangled Et'moru lying in the snow.

"Let me look at ye," MacShaka said as he pulled out a medi-kit. "We've nae time tae make you pretty," he remarked as I spied Bohman and the four remaining *Athand'u* standing with the rifles at the high port. "Ye're bleedin' but we need tae gaet movin'." He slapped a bio-dressing on my head and pushed me towards my trembling tundra camel. "Gaet movin'," he ordered as he mounted his own tundra camel. He tapped the comm bud in his ear. "Cong, gaet the fucking contubernium down here and watch yerself. There are fucking *Et'moru* in the woods."

"How was that, hoss?" Bonham asked wide-eyed and panting with a grin beneath that massive moustache. "That bugger jumped on you faster than a duck on a june bug!" I swear the nuggety little idiot was laughing at me, bleeding and crying my eyes out from fear that I was. Bellona, herself bloodied and limping, led us up the track until nearly 10 minutes later, Cong and his contubernium came barrelling down to meet us. With them covering our back, we continued up the trail until we burst into open field with the convent and its locked gates and well armed nuns looking at us from the windows. The gates opened and our rag tag column trotted in.

"Off ye gaet, lad," MacShaka said as he *kooshed* my camel and helped me off. I was weak from loss of blood and fear, and I sank to my knees in a faint.

"Lad," he said with a chuckle as he picked me up in his burly arms, "ye've mair luck in ye than I thought possible. I need ye tae pick lottery numbers for me one day. Sure I'll be a rich man and off this rock."

With those words sounding distant in my ears, I closed my eyes and fainted.

Part Seven

Fight This Day The Battle of The Lord

"Sit up, lad, and quit yer whining," MacShaka huffed as he brushed gore off my face. He held a bio-dressing package in his teeth as he used both hands to hold my face and look at the gashes with a critical eye.

"Hoss," Bohman said as he stood beside MacShaka, "looks like you was pulled through a knothole backwards." A smile formed and he added, "After yer mornin', ye could sit on a fence and have the birds feed ye."

That one even stumped MacShaka who paused in fondling my face like a polar bear and looked at Bohman with a quizzical eye. "Losh, awa' wi' ye, auld yin," he said through his clenched teeth.

We were back in my room and I was sitting on the bed with a face slashed cruelly. It hurt, though less so after a dose of laudanum from the nuns. The pain had dulled enough so that my tears were far fewer than they had been 30 minutes earlier when I came out of my faint with the contubernium huddled around me and looking pensive. MacShaka had sent them packing – especially a weepy-eyed Jindan and a raging Usman – ordering them to man the windows and watch for the *Et'moru*.

The *Et'moru*.

The memory of that dreadful moment when the creature held my face in its ferocious grip and our eyes connected – mine wide with terror and hers orange and bold with an unspeakable malevolence. I would have been dead if not for MacShaka.

"Here, hauld still, ye soor faced keelie," he grunted as he held the side of my head in his massive paw, wiped away more blood, and applied the bio-dressing. "Damned thing nearly tore yer ear off," he joked with a hollow grin. "Jindan weel no' find ye near as bonnie as ye were a few days back."

"That's not funny," I whined between sniffles and wiping my nose.

"Aye it is," MacShaka responded while wagging his finger under my broken nose. "An' I tell ye this much, Sikunder, I'm gaetin some tired o' patching up yer keelie hide. Between ye gaettin' cut, shot, and broken these last few months, I'm mair yer God damned medic than yer subedar." His smile widened until he looked like an amused buffalo.

"Learn tae duck yer fucking heid."

"I will, huzūra," I replied amidst fresh tears.

"Och, lad," MacShaka said in mild disgust as he wiped my gore off his hands. "Ye already hae a bumfle face now, dinnae make it worse wi' all the blubberin'. Ye're alive," he said with a sudden earnestness, "that's mair that can be said for some."

He had me there, so I took every effort to sort myself out. The bio-dressing lessened the pain further, and when MacShaka handed me a mirror, I looked upon myself for the first time since I had left the castrum days before.

I was shocked into silence.

I was 17 years old, yet I had the face of a man three times my age. My shaven head had several days of stubble; one ear – the one nearly torn off – was misshapen and sitting a little lower than before beneath the dressings; my broken nose was now pushed back into place framed by eyes that were black and swollen; and I had a livid gash on my jawline beneath the fine down of my beard and moustache. He was right, I looked horrible.

MacShaka sat back and sipped a cooling mug of coffee. He seemed affable enough, even after the events of the day so I posed a question that had been on my mind since the discovery of the slaughtered *Athand'u*.

"*Huzūra*, what did you mean when you said 'it all made sense now'?"

MacShaka emerged from deep contemplation and his unfocused eyes swung to me and a grim countenance formed. "Aye, weel, lad, it all made sense tae me; the story o' the *Et'moru* o' course. Ye see," he explained as he sat back and crossed his beefy arms, "what the *Athand'u* told us didnae make much sense, really, which was why I was loathe tae believe them. Now that they hae been killed by the *Et'moru*, weel it begins tae add up. The *Athand'u* are the largest tribe in the gleann, about 200 or mair, and a threat tae the *Et'moru* wha' hae moved in. Your attack on the *Chúsheng*," he added with a touch of severity, "and Bohman's column, were Godsends tae the *Et'moru* wha' were smart enough tae use them as signs that the Legion and Constabulary were about tae move intae the valley and sort out the Gliesiuns and *Chúsheng* alike. They convinced the *Athand'u* that attacking the column was the right move, and it did two things. Fairst, a column o' Terrans was eliminated without any risk tae the *Et'moru*, and secondly, it established some kind o' trust between the *Et'moru* and the *Athand'u*; enough at least for the *Athand'u* tae lower their guard. Now, lad, the *Et'moru* have removed two o' the biggest threats tae their presence here and there's only one left between them and wholesale slaughter here."

"The Legion?" I asked.

"Och," MacShaka looked disgusted, "gae bile yer heid and make daft soup. The Legion weel no' come in here if it doesnae hae tae – the company weel ensure that – nor the Constabulary. Too damned expensive tae send in columns tae fight in a gleann no' even recognized as a settlement by the UN."

"That's ridiculous," I retorted. "So what if the gleann isn't classified as a settlement? There are still Terrans being killed by Gliesiuns – which is what the Legion is supposed to ensure does not happen."

"Within the colony," MacShaka replied with surprising patience. "It's a wee clause in the contract. Everyone knew that when settlement began, it would move far faster than planned. If the Legion and Constabulary tried to keep pace, it would send the costs skyrocketing. Think o' it, lad, every time settlers decided tae take up residence in a new valley and we followed with more castrums filled with jawans and constables to protect them, the Company would hae tae pay for that. That clause was put in there tae ensure that if settlers moved beyond the Company's plans, it was at their ain risk. Gleann Ceallach falls beyond Company plans even if Bohman did send a column in and he'll pay fer that wi' his job, ye can bet on that."

"And you? What will the Legion do to you now that you're in here?"

"Me?" MacShaka considered my question for a moment before a smile formed. "Och, no' a thing. I'm here on Legion orders tae remove the bodies. It's no' my fault if the weather has held us here longer than we wanted."

"So, if it's not the Legion that stands between the *Et'moru* and the valley, who is it?"

"Ye need tae ask, lad?" MacShaka asked with some surprise. "It's the Cardinal herself. That nippie-sweetie is the real power in this valley and the *Et'moru* weel hae fingered that out by now. This convent weel be the next target and soon."

That didn't make me feel any better – not one bit.

"How soon?"

MacShaka shrugged. "I hope very soon. I'll no' be able tae delay here long. Once the weather breaks, I'll hae tae return tae the castrum and leave the wee miserable carline here on her ain. I doubt she'll survive it. With myself and Bohman here, however, and wi' the last of the *Athand'u*, we just might be able tae hauld them off; depends on their numbers though."

"And do we know how many there are?"

"A hundred or more," MacShaka returned. "That's what that bitch Bellona believes."

A hundred or more of the most homicidal creatures in existence whose fearlessness and hatred were legendary, I thought with growing horror. Standing against them were a hundred or so nuns, about 20 jawans, a half dozen constables, and a score of *Athand'u*.

Those were terrible odds.

MacShaka stood up and clapped his hands against the cold. "Get some rest, lad, then come on out and hae a bite. We'll hae company soon enough and even your pulse rifle may come in handy."

* * * * *

"So let me just get this straight," Bohman exclaimed as he sipped coffee and looked at MacShaka with surprise, "we're stayin' on as long as decently possible with our fingers crossed that those no-account sons o' bitches attack us in force?"

"Aye," MacShaka replied as he puffed on his pipe.

It was just the jawans and constables in the common room – the nuns were again at prayer and the *Athand'u* were in the courtyard. There were 26 of us sitting around the tables before the roaring fire, and each face was a mask of worry and fear at the thought of the coming of the *Et'moru*.

"Fact is," MacShaka continued, "I've talked wi' our bimbashi, and even Amir Shao Zhong-qi. They in turn, hae talked wi' Governor Jefferson and she has gone right tae the United Nations Department of Colonial Affairs and Klondikecorp's Board of Directors and even Klondikecorp's Colonial Operations Council. There isnae anyone in the Company nor the UNDCA wha's interested in the Legion getting involved wi' a scrap outside o' UN controlled territory, and Gleann Ceallach is outside UNDCA controlled territory. If the *Et'moru* could be convinced tae invade Aebbas Vallis, this part o' the problem would just gae away."

"Those sons o' bitches may be so low as to have to look up to see hell," Bohman interrupted, "but they're as smart as a hooty owl. They might oughta have a pretty good idea that our tepid response to the loss of my column means we're about as shy as sapphires out here."

MacShaka stared at him blankly for a moment and I crowed inside. See how you like it, I thought.

"Aye, weel," he resumed, "the point is, there's nae help for the gleann." He pointed his pipe stem at Bohman. "Your damned column shouldnae hae been in here anyway, but there wasnae a man alive who thought they'd be rubbed out by *Athand'u* at the fucking behest of the *Et'moru*; sae now we hae a problem." MacShaka looked at each face. "If we leave, it is my belief that the *Et'moru* weel wipe this place out. I think if we stay, they'll attack anyway, but this gang o' she-bears weel stand a better chance." He again paused and looked at each of us. "It's my decision that we stay."

"Didn't you just finish tellin' us that there wasn't a single person in the UN and the Company who was in agreement with our stayin'?" Bohman asked with a wink.

"Aye, but I couldnae care a docken fer what the Company wants. Besides," he added with a grin. "We're snowed in and the Governor and the Amir know it."

"Thick as fleas on a farm dog ye are," Bohman replied with a sour grin. "Seems like we're burnin' daylight if'n we're goin' to be stickin' around an' spoilin' fer a fight."

"Agreed. Havildars, sort yer keelies out, post sentries, set up a powerpack recharge station and a medical station fer the wounded; off ye gae."

I made to stand and Sittina waved me off. "Sit down and rest a while longer," she said as she perused me with a motherly mien. "You're not much use anyway and the last thing we need is you fainting away again." She smiled and bullied her diminished contubernium while Muneer hauled away a grinning Usman by the ear. In moments, the common room had emptied save for MacShaka, Bohman, and myself.

"Well, hoss," Bohman said to me after a long silence where he sipped coffee and puffed on his pipe, "you look about as nervous as a fly in a glue pot. Not much point of that really," he drawled, "a day or so from now you'll either be back snug and safe in your castrum or you'll have swapped yer guitar fer a harp." He chuckled, a deep cackling that brought a painful smile to my face.

"Och, Bohman," MacShaka growled as he shook his head in disbelief. A grin formed and he said, "Ye'll terrify the lad wi' yer capers."

"Terrify?" Bohman replied as he tipped his Stetson. "This boy Sikunder? Hell, he's braver than the first fella what ate an oyster, and he'd charge hell with no more'n a bucket of ice water. And that's a fact."

Well, it brought a flush of pleasure to have that old law dog talking such foolishness. I know most of it was rubbish to try and make me feel a bit better, but the fact he felt compelled suggested that he cared. MacShaka said nothing as he stood and motioned for Bohman to follow.

"You stay here for a bit longer lad, but dinnae ye dog it tae long; Muneer doesnae have the patience of Sittina. Ye're lucky Erhong wasnae here when you were jumped. She might hae killed the *Et'moru* and then you just fer bein' alive." That got the old goat chuckling and with that, he and Bohman left.

I took the opportunity to sit near the fire, play with the dressing around my ear for a bit, and revel in the pain meds that were making my brain foggy and turning my body to pudding. It also gave me the opportunity to muse at my lot; once again I was in a life and death scenario with the death side of it looking far more likely. I'd had a few days of utter terror, though surprisingly, I had been able to shake it off far better than I expected. Oh my guts were still churning at the thought of my very brief future, and I was in a sweat with the thought that I could once again be hand to hand with one of those creatures, but it seemed different than those earlier times. When I'd stormed the beach in Coloe Vallis, I couldn't run away fast enough, and although I ran from Lukianos, it had been an unconscious move, not the more conscious decision I had made on that beach that given the chance, I'd flee. (I didn't by the way; I'd not had the chance as Sittina had grabbed me by the scruff and dragged me from my hidey hole into the breach, damn her.)

I felt different now. Although I was still plagued by guilt I felt a sliver of real confidence. It was odd, to feel such conflicting emotions, and yet after six months of hellish existence on Samsāra I was slowly maturing from terrified and useless to mostly terrified and not quite so useless. A bold estimation, I know, but it was true.

* * * * *

The coffee was long gone and I had lit up a pipe full of *bhang* to help with the pain and my nerves when the door from the courtyard opened and Coulthard entered. She wore a mantle over her cassock and scapular and her head was shadowed in the cowl. She pulled it back, shaking the snow off, before she came to stand before the fire. Her mien was severe – her lips pursed and eyes distant. Her long grey braided topknot fell behind her ear and down the front of her tunic as she warmed her backside and hands with the fire. Facing me, she finally looked at me, and those cold grey eyes softened slightly.

"*Bhang*, Sikunder?" she growled as I lowered the pipe. "*A diabolo, qui est simia dei.*"

"Sorry," I replied feeling sheepish.

"Where God has a church the Devil will have his chapel, Sikunder. Now put that out this instant. Jesus never resorted to puffing on a pipe full of bhang when he was having a bad day!"

I did as I was told, knocking the embers into the fire before resuming my seat at the table.

"Now," she said in a slightly more conciliatory tone, "how are you, Sikunder?"

I wiped my nose and replied, "I'm okay; ear hurts though."

"I should think," she replied in clipped tones. "*Beware of entrance to a quarrel, but being in, bear 't that th' opposèd may beware of thee. Give every man thy ear but few thy voice.*"

Silence followed while I sat confused. A small smile crossed her lips. "It is Shakespeare, Sikunder, from Hamlet."

"Ah," I replied with all of the mouth breathing literary credibility of a cow.

"You are unfamiliar with Shakespeare," she said as she took a seat beside me. "What a sad state of affairs for public education."

"I was pretty good at math," I admitted.

"Math lacks nuances," Coulthard said as she sat back in a wooden chair, her eyes drawn to the crackling flames. "It's a scientist's language, one better used for cold impersonal conversations that discuss expostulate quantum chromodynamics or loop quantum gravity. It is the language of the emotionally detached," she chided as she stretched her legs out. "God enjoys math, but he speaks in Latin," she added severely. "*Cuiusvis hominis est errare, nullius nisi insipientis in errore perseverare.*"

"What does that mean?"

She spared me a frosty glance and a thin smile. "Any man can make a mistake; only a fool keeps making the same one."

"I see." I didn't, though, as I pawed at my bandages. I wondered if she was trying to be clever at the expense of my wounded face.

Coulthard brought her thin hands before her and slowly rubbed warmth into them. "I hear you are staying for a bit," she observed.

"Yes."

"I must admit, that initially, I was not enthused with the idea. Jawans and constables in this convent may not be an affront to God or Brigid, but it is possible that they may not be impressed." She paused and I wondered at her reasoning. "However, I was reminded by my own words to you that day you awoke with the name of your friend on your lips."

"Lukianos," I whispered.

"Yes." She replied. Her voice was curt and I found myself shrinking away from her. "Your subedar and the warden have agreed to a possible sacrifice if things do not work out for us. There are 26 of you, and although you may not all be volunteers," a thin smile crossed her lips when she looked at me, "it is a still a willing sacrifice after a fashion. Who am I to refuse such complete generosity?"

"You could leave." I volunteered. "Pack everyone up and go. We might escape."

"I doubt that, Sikunder."

"It's worth a try," I persisted.

Coulthard shook her head. "*To move is to stir, and to be valiant is to stand; therefore, if thou art mov'd, thou runst away.*"

"More Shakespeare?" I asked. She nodded.

"MacBeth, though I should think you know that. Any jawan worth his salt should have read MacBeth," she said with a sniff and edge to her voice. She relented, however. "No, Sikunder," she said, "we would never reach the castrum. Your subedar and I actually discussed it. Our position is best if we stay here."

"Won't the *Et'moru* just attack Svarga?"

Coulthard considered the question. "They might, but your subedar seems to think otherwise. So does Bellona."

"So we're the preferred target," I sighed.

"Yes." Coulthard was silent for several moments while I glanced longingly at my pipe. "However, I have faith that we will prevail."

"Why?"

Coulthard smiled. "Faith, jawan, is the reality of things hoped for, the evidence of things not seen."

"What does that mean?" I asked.

"It is my belief that when we have hope, true hope, that faith in God changes that hope to reality. My hope is that we will survive an attack from the *Et'moru* and in turn, defeat them and end their threat to us and the settlers of this gleann. That hope is a true hope, and I have a true faith in God that he will take that hope, and through my faith, make it a reality. I will stand before the *Et'moru* and I will be brave and I will fight. I will defeat them."

"I wish I had your faith," I quavered.

"That is for you to find. *For by grace are ye saved through faith; and that not of yourselves: it is the gift of Brigid.*"

"Are you not afraid?" I asked. I certainly was; those horrible orange eyes and that horrible hatred.

"I am very afraid," Coulthard replied. She pulled out a rosary.
"*Hail Mary, full of grace, the Lord is with thee;
blessed art thou among women, and blessed is the fruit of thy womb,
Jesus.
Holy Mary, Mother of God, pray for us sinners,
now and at the hour of our death. Amen.*"

"Are we at the hour of our death?" I asked. A wane smile crossed Coulthard's narrow face.

"*Hora mortis.* Yes."

A few moments passed where I felt tears welling in self pity. I couldn't see how I could get out of this one. At least when I charged the Tongs in Coloe Vallis, I had 250 jawans and another 100 Neo Celts at my back. As unlikely as it was that I'd live through that hellfire, the odds at least had been about 50/50 that morning. Not so today. We had maybe 100 rifles at our hand, three quarters of them held by untrained nuns. Yes, it was enough to make me weep; the thought of 100 or more *Et'moru* punching through the gates and falling upon us with all of their fanatical fury. Suddenly I felt her cold hand, little more than a collection of

162

dry bones wrapped in cool skin, grasp mine. I glanced at her, but she was staring deep into the fire. "*O, but they say the tongues of dying men enforce attention like deep harmony: where words are scarce, they are seldom spent in vain, for they breathe truth that breathe their words in pain. He that no more must say is listen'd more than they whom youth and ease have taught to glose; more are men's ends mark'd than their lives before.*"

She gripped my hand tighter.

"When I was 22, Sikunder," she said in a soft dirge, "I was a missionary in Tajikistan. I worked in a UN camp, helping refugees from China's civil war that had gone nuclear when I was an infant. I fed refugees in the kitchen tent, helped by nursing in the hospital tent, and taught the children English. I did this for six months before I was kidnapped by members of a criminal gang that stalked the camp. They held me in a tent many kilometres from what little civilization you could find in that hellish country, and every night, they raped me. Even after I became pregnant, they continued with the rape until one day, I had a child, a boy whom I never named. He was taken and I never saw him again. In the weeks after, I believe they finally tired of me and one morning two of them took me out into the countryside to kill me. They placed me on my knees while they argued amongst themselves who would have the pleasure of shooting me in the head."

I felt my stomach churn and shivers ran down my back.

"As I prayed to Jesus to give me the strength to face my death, I had a vision – a visitation from Saint Brigid. She was magnificent; luminous in her beauty and terrible in her righteous fury. She was angry with me and scolded me for my inaction. She praised my efforts with the refugees and my endurance while a prisoner, but she berated me for kneeling there and waiting to die. She said, '*Stand and fight, daughter of God. I will be with you so that you may courageously fight and wholly vanquish your enemies! I and the holy angels will refuse them mercy!* And so, I reached out before me as my executioners argued, and I grabbed two large stones. I turned and threw the first one, hitting one of the men in the face. The other stood transfixed for a moment, and I leapt and fell upon him in a berserk fury and beat him to death with the second stone. The first man was stunned, but as he recovered and made to stand, I took the pistol from the man I had just killed, and shot him in the head."

"My God," I whispered.

"I walked back to a refugee camp and resumed my work. I never looked back and Saint Brigid has stood by my side ever since biding me not to stand idle, but to fight. Always fight, especially when the odds are at their highest against you. That is the strength God wishes you to seek, Sikunder." She pulled her gaze from the fire and fixed her eyes upon me. "Today, I will stand side by side with Saint Brigid as I did in the desert over 40 years ago and I will face the *Et'moru* as they come through the gates. Today, she will call me home, and today I will gladly go with her. You, Sikunder, may stand by my side if you wish."

We lapsed into silence – her to pray and me to fret. I'm not sure that I hadn't somehow accepted the fact that the odds were damned good that I wouldn't get out of that convent alive. My parents, whom I'd only told a week before where I was, would soon receive that institutional missive, *'The United Nations is sorry to report the loss of your son in some out of the way hole in the colony of Samsāra...'* or some such thing.

I'm still here of course, 50 years later, but that day as the snow fell and we hunkered down for the expected attack that would wipe us from existence, well, I felt that my time was nearly up. After Coulthard left, I took a few minutes to record a final message to my parents on my compu-pad, and when it was done, I uploaded it with a 48 hour time lag that, if I didn't stop it, would send it out on the next data packet. I actually forgot about it in the aftermath of events, and my parents received a video from their son, battered and bloody in a darkened hall in a convent 20 light years from Earth explaining how he had died at the hands of a murderous tribe of Gliesiuns called the *Et'moru*. I was in their bad books for months after that, but I think they finally realized the danger their son was in.

* * * * *

"Sae listen up," MacShaka said as he looked upon his jawans and Bohman's constables now gathered again in the common room again, "we hae only a wee bit o' time left afore those miserable murderin' nippit bastards show up tae dae us a bit o' harm. We need tae secure this place as best as possible and that means sentries at the windows and some o' ye cuttin' out new holes on the second floor. We need the gates reinforced and we need fire buckets spread out." Usman chuckled and nudged Fung Wai-ting who pointedly ignored him. "That keelie," MacShaka said as he pointed at Usman and used his official hanging judge voice, "can get his sorry arse up ontae the roof tae keep an eye out!"

Everyone chuckled and Usman, smiling for a moment until he realized MacShaka was as serious as a bishop talking salvation, lost his grin and moved off to a room with a ladder that led to the roof.

MacShaka was at his prime now, a bellicose martinet who had chosen his fate, and like that day so many months before when he had stepped off a paddlewheeler singing Johnnie Cope and marched – not ran, but marched – up the beach to charge the

Black Hand trenches, well you get a bit of an idea of what he was like with a full head of martial steam for a task. The task, of course, was to survive an assault by the *Et'moru*. Coulthard and MacShaka, even our Amir and the Governor, each knew without a doubt that this terrible band of Gliesiuns would unleash their hatred upon us, and save leaving the 26 jawans and constables in a valley where they didn't have any jurisdiction nor responsibility, there wasn't much more they could do. The fate of hundreds was in the balance now; the nuns, the settlement of Svarga, and the families up and down the valley. Word was out; for a pair of Bellona's warriors had linked up with the few dozen *Tasyage* and the *Ech'cha* to pass the warning, racing up and down the valley chivvying as many to Svarga or the castrum as possible.

We put that out of our minds now as we prepared. My job was minor enough as I set up a recharge station in the common room for our pulse rifle power packs as well as a printing station for bullets. It was mindless work, feeding in packets of granular material to pump out 100 rounds per minute. Mindless, it was, but terribly important since we'd only packed 100 rounds per person and the odds were that we'd need so much more in the coming fight. The nuns, armed Boadiceas that they were, had little real ammo and only one very slow recharging station. However, the equipment we had brought – and MacShaka had shown keen foresight in bringing it – meant that we were in good shape for ammunition at least.

The nuns spent their time prepping a surgery and recovery room, for no one had any illusions that we would emerge unbloodied. Here we were poorer, but we made due with torn up sheets and laudanum to supplement the medikits the Legion had brought. As time passed and my work was done for the moment with every powerpack fully charged, all magazines loaded, and

166

several hundred rounds held back for reloads, I opted to tour the preparations while warming myself with a jug of hot tea to share, and soothing my nerves with a pipe full of *bhang*.

The second floor was a hive of activity as nuns and jawans manned the windows while also cutting out new firing slits in the walls as well as murder holes above the gate. They were also bringing in the cordwood and stacking it around the windows like sandbags, for it was unknown how well the *Et'moru* were armed.

"You can bet that they took the trade rifles of the *Athand'u, Enna lillah wa enna elaihe Rajioun*," said Muneer as he stacked wood beneath a window. He had stripped down to his *kurta* and a black skullcap, and even in the cold that pervaded the room, he had worked up a sweat. "That means, jawan," he said as he paused to focus on me with eyes long touched by madness, "that when they come, they will be well armed as well as bloodthirsty." He paused and took the cup of tea I offered. He raised it, looked up and said, "*A-ozu billahi mena shaitaan Arrajeem*," then sipped the scalding tea.

"What does that mean?" I asked, dreading the answer I might receive. We were close to death, however, and I thought that earned me the right to query our mad mullah. He tightened his lips and raised his hand to strike, but suddenly thought better of it.

"It means, *I seek refuge in Allah from the cursed Shaitan*," he replied. "It is said by a Muslim when he feels unsafe." It was one of those rare admissions by that maniac, a man who had once been a mullah in Syria until some event of unknown depravity had pushed him into the Off-World Legion. It was impossible to discern what that event might have been – no one seemed to know – though there was plenty of speculation, everything from pedophilia to sneaking around with some politician's daughter to coupling with a goat (that was Usman's idea). I didn't dare ask, however. It was enough that I had the *Et'moru* trying to kill me.

"What is that you stare at?" he asked with sudden pique while finishing his tea. "You have the eyes of a cod and the brains of a worm, Sikunder," he said with a derisive sniff. "*Ibn Al-Himar*," he added as an afterthought.

Well, I knew that one well enough. 'Son of a Donkey' was nearly my nickname with him, and sensing that the end of our polite *palaver* had come, I decided I'd move on.

"The tea was most welcome, *Alhamdulillah*," he said with a certain pleasantness that took me aback. "*Shokran*."

"You're welcome," I replied, once again unsure of what had just transpired with the man.

I walked past a half dozen Gliesiuns, bringing wood up from the courtyard, to find Sittina, Fung Wai-ting, and Yee Hong-miao musing over who should take a sentry position at a window.

"Both of you are *bái mù*, and I'm not sure I can leave either one of you here," Sittina said as she crossed her arms and looked severe. Neither Wai-ting nor Hong-miao bought it, though they did manage to look somewhat meek as they hid their little smiles. "Sikunder," Sittina said as she took a cup of tea. "Who would you put here if you had your druthers?"

"Me," I replied with a bit of sauce. The girls giggled as I poured them tea and Sittina pursed her lips.

"Nonsense," she said before taking another sip. "You're too busy charging power packs and printing bullets."

"All done," I said as I puffed on my pipe. The *bhang* was giving me that much desired warmth and calmness of spirit that I needed before the coming of battle. Sittina had it spades without the use of drugs, lucky for her.

"You smoke too much of that stiff, Sikunder, and it'll be *shén jīng bìng* for you."

"Better that than sane and terrified, *sahiba*," I replied. The girls tittered and Sittina jerked her thumb for me to leave.

"If you're not here to help, then grab the teapot and keep moving." I walked past her and she added, "I'm glad you're spoiling for a fight. We're going to need you."

Well, I wasn't really spoiling for a fight, but I had certainly accepted the fact that it was coming. With evening approaching and the snow thinning to flurries, the odds were good that the *Et'moru* would be here shortly. I went below and found Bohman by the main gate, his constables having secured the entrance with additional boards as well as laying out obstacles that would slow the *Et'moru* if they managed to get through. I handed the old Texas Ranger a cup of tea at which he sniffed, made a face, and then asked, "What the hell is this?"

"Coca tea," I replied fighting a smirk.

"God damn it, hoss, it's cold as a cast iron commode and all you have is tea? What the hell is Coca tea anyway?"

"It's a leaf. Cocaine comes from it."

"Cocaine?" Bohman was working his way towards amused fury. "Here I am, near about past going, and instead o' bringin' me coffee so strong that it'll walk into my cup, you bring me tea. Tea! I need something hot as a pot of neck bones, hoss, to fight the damned cold!"

Bohman had a wide grin on him now, and I pulled a thermos from my bag. "Fine then," I said as I poured him a cup of hot strong coffee. "This stuff is hotter than the hinges of hell," I added in my best Texas twang.

"Hoss, you're lucky you got that thermos. You speakin' 10 words a second with them gusts to 50 will get you into trouble."

"Are we set?" I asked as I motioned my cup towards the gate.

"What, that gate? Hell no, hoss." He smiled beneath his massive moustache. "That gate's about as useless as two buggies in a one horse town. Hell, all we could do is put some planks over them and stack a pile of junk in from of them. The *Et'moru* will be faster through 'em than double struck lightning, and that's a fact."

"How do we plan to hold them back?" I begged with a new pit forming in my stomach.

"Well, hoss, that there is fer the nuns to sort out. Mama superior there said she and her girls'll hold the line here, and since she's as tough as stewed skunk, well, I believe her."

I did too, but Bohman's honest appraisal of our chances wasn't helping my nerves one bit. Of course, MacShaka had an answer to that an hour later.

"Grab yer stuff, Sikunder. Since ye're the only keelie sittin' on his arse horn idle and useless, you can come out wi' me to look about the perimeter."

I was as near refusing the brute as I ever had been. I was stunned of course, the idea of leaving the gates and the extremely modest safety of the convent to go tooling around in the darkness looking for the most murderous Gliesiun tribe in history smacked of insanity, and if the order hadn't come from a man the size of a polar bear with the personality of a crocodile, I would have told him to stuff his order and take my chances.

I wasn't that stupid though, even if it did mean a horrific death at the hands of the *Et'moru*. You see, as much as I was afraid of the *Et'moru*, I was clearly afraid of MacShaka just a little bit more.

So, 10 minutes later, MacShaka led myself, Bohman and one of his constables – a young scrawny Libyan named al-Sanussi, if I recall correctly – out of the gates just blocked and into the dusk for a walk around the perimeter. As the perimeter was located 100 or so meters from the convent, it meant a decent trek through snow that was calf deep. With our tactical contact lenses we had thermal vision so the darkness meant nothing save for its more traditional and sinister role of housing the unknown. It felt to me, as we slogged through the snow with our rifles at the ready, that eyes were watching our ponderous progress as the deep darkness made its final descent upon us. Of course with our tactical lenses engaged, we didn't experience the full extent of the night, but for a moment, as we paused for a breath, I succumbed to the innate curiosity of my youth and turned off my lenses for a few seconds. The darkness that enfolded me was utterly complete, so much so that even the hand-in-front-of-my-face cliché was horrifically accurate, and I promptly ordered them back on, much to my relief.

It took us perhaps an hour to complete the tour, and freezing cold it was that night with the temperature dipping well below -20. That meant light flurries only and toes that nothing seemed to warm even though I was well dressed for the weather. As we paused beside a tree stump and MacShaka reported to Sittina and Cong, Bohman squatted beside me and said through chattering teeth, "Colder than a frosted frog, tonight," he said beneath a moustache thick with ice. "Betcha it gets even colder before long."

"I don't want to think about it," I replied in a whisper. My eyes were furtively scanning the abyssal darkness of the tree line, and as Bohman and al-Sanussi muttered amongst themselves, I saw the briefest of illuminations deep within.

"I saw something," I hissed as close to a yelp as I could. MacShaka stopped speaking as I brought my rifle up.

"Dinnae shoot, ye daft gomeril!" MacShaka mouth as he grabbed my rifle. "Whaur abouts daed ye see it?"

I pointed in the direction, my gloved hand shaking in fear, and MacShaka nodded and signalled us to follow. I thought for a moment that he must have made a mistake; no human with even a hardly sound mind would take four men towards what was likely an *Et'moru* horde. I tried to explain my feelings once to my future wife, and it went something like this:

Me: "And so, I thought that MacShaka was clearly off his rocker to lead us towards an army of Et'moru."

Wife: "Dear," she said abstracted, she was trying to learn how to knit, "didn't you say there were a hundred or more maybe, or that you didn't actually know? How is that an army?"

Me: a little annoyed by her rather pedantic response – "It's not really important whether an army existed or not, it was the assumption I made that we, all four of us, were going towards an army, my love."

Wife: "Knit one, pearl two... damn it, I did it again. Here, hold this for a moment, dear," as she handed me the ball of yarn, "but you did say army, my dear, which is what I'm not following. Why would you use that term when in fact, you were not going towards an army. It's not like they had tanks and airplanes, right dear?"

There were times when my wife, with her PhD in economics, truly surprised me. Me: "No, my dear, at least, I don't recall seeing them driving in tanks, which is odd when you think about it, because one would have thought we would have seen tracks."

Wife: "And the airplanes, dear?"

Me: "Yes, it's possible we missed those."

Wife: "So, it sounds a bit like an exaggeration, dear."

Me: "Yes, you may be right, dear. I suppose, as we made our way to what we perceived as certain death, and I mean a beheading and spreading of our bodies over the better part of a hectare..."

Wife: "Please, dear, don't be crude. I've put the kettle on you know and I have fresh biscuits."

Me: "Apologies, my dear. Yes, I suppose it might have been an exaggeration. Yes, you are right."

This was often how my harrowing tales of life and death were met when I attempted to entertain my wife.

So we entered the woods, moving cautiously in the darkness, our breath held as we chose each step while our eyes pierced the gloom for any sign. Bohman had the rear as MacShaka led us deeper into the forest, and he paused to watch our rear while al-Sanussi seemed almost to be in my back pocket. Each step wrenched further thoughts that what we were doing was absolute madness, and it took physical effort not climb a stump so I could grab MacShaka by his collar and shake him while shrieking, "What the fuck are you thinking of?" I didn't of course, for had I survived the event, the *Et'moru* would have surely killed us.

MacShaka bade us pause after we'd gone about 100 meters or so in, and we squatted behind a fallen log, our rifles resting on the thick layer of snow while we scanned the murk beyond. There was nothing save the ghostly images of tall trees with a carpet of brush and bracken beneath a thick blanket of snow.

"Maybe I was seeing things," I admitted in a hush. MacShaka didn't answer for nearly a minute.

"Och, they're out here, lad. I can hear them."

I wondered at that, for to me there had been a deep silence save for our heavy breathing and the occasional soft snap of a stick beneath our cautious footsteps. No sooner had MacShaka said that, however, than I heard a distant shriek in the darkness – a vicious cry of hatred and malice – answered by another to the north of us.

"Aye, they're movin' in," MacShaka said. "Surroundin' us."

"I'm all fer lookin' about for these animals, but ya'll oughta whistle before you walk into a stranger's camp," Bohman remarked.

"Aye," MacShaka replied, as if he actually understood the Texan. "We'll head back." It was only a hundred meters or so to the tree line and the open land around the convent, but it felt like 10 kilometres, for if we were slow moving and cautious before, we were doubly so now in order to avoid detection. We'd been moving perhaps a minute when we heard a new cry, this time closer and to the south of us. MacShaka bade us halt, and we peered keenly into the darkness. No movement, no thermal image, but the *Et'moru* were clearly closing the distance. MacShaka tapped his earbud and whispered orders to Sittina. "I think," he said as he turned to look at us, "that we may need to pick up the pace a wee bit."

There was fear in him, and I knew right then and there that MacShaka's cockiness had gotten us into trouble. We were still some distance from the convent and the *Et'moru* were in the woods. "Bohman," he whispered. "You and yer peeler lead the way. Sikunder, right behind them, and I'll bring up the rear."

There was a barely discernable tremble in MacShaka's voice, but it was enough to bring me as near as not to wetting myself.

"Move out," MacShaka hissed.

We ploughed through the snow, kicking up powder into a fine haze as we leapt over snow covered logs and brush. We could see the convent now through the thinning trees, and it took every effort not to simply drop my rifle and pack, and sprint the last 50 meters.

"Hauld up!" MacShaka whispered. He dropped to one knee and brought his rifle up. I did the same but Bohman and al-Sanussi hadn't heard; they continued on. "God damn it," MacShaka grunted. I suddenly saw what he was looking at – a shimmering beast nearly 50 meters to the north emerging from brush. Although difficult to discern, it was obvious that it had seen Bohman and al-Sanussi, for it let out a terrific shriek and bounded through the snow towards them.

"Now's the time!" MacShaka roared as he stood. He fired, his pulse rifle bucking as it sent rounds towards the loping *Et'moru*. "Run, Bohman!" MacShaka bellowed. "Dinnae ye look back!" There were more creatures in the woods, and a few shots rang out. "Watch yer targets, Sikunder! Move!"

I was terrified. It was the ambush all over again, perhaps worse this time as I knew what fate awaited me if I was captured. My heart was pumping to explode, my breathing was ragged and gasping, and I thought I'd faint, piss myself, or throw up. I stumbled through the snow with MacShaka at my feet urging me forward while the shrieks around us increased.

"Hauld up and pick a target!" MacShaka said as he turned and fired.

I looked briefly through my tear filled eyes, saw a luminescent shape moving across my vision, brought up my rifle to my heaving chest and fired. I have no idea if I hit anything, but MacShaka shoved me from behind.

"Get movin'!" he barked.

The snow slowed us and it was tiring as we pushed through calf high drifts. The trees further thinned and suddenly we were in the clear and moving as quickly as we could to the convent.

"Hauld up and fire behind!" MacShaka called out.

I spun, dropped to a knee and fired into the darkness of the forest with its flitting luminescent shapes. The shrieks were growing in intensity and at least one sounded like it was driven more from pain than hate.

"Gae on, lad!" MacShaka said as he pulled me by the scruff.

Again we were punching through the snow, but this time I could hear the 'snap' of rounds fanning past us. They were firing from the convent, and the open doors with the dull light of fires beyond penetrating the horrible darkness was the most inviting sight I had ever seen.

"Move yer keelie arse, Sikunder," MacShaka urged.

More shots rang out and suddenly we were through the gate and collapsing onto the snow in the courtyard. There were a score of nuns chattering around us while Sittina and Cong raged, and Bohman sat with al-Sanussi and glared daggers at MacShaka.

The big yin himself lay on his back, breathing like a bellows and coughing before he sat up with shoulders shaking in sudden mirth. He looked at me, tried to speak, but dissolved into another fit of giggles.

"Jesus, what is it?" I gasped.

He was still laughing when he laid a massive paw on my knee, took a deep breath and said, "Och, lad, ye were such a beauty when ye was runnin'!" He giggled even harder before he added, "There's aye a something when ye gae out intae a fight. Best remember the important parts in order tae save yer scalp."

"What important parts?" I asked.

"Lad, I forgot that the damned things can see in the dark." He started laughing again and fell on his back.

"How the fuck do you forget that?" I shrieked. Any caution that I might have wisely displayed disappeared with the notion that we barely escaped death, and that I would have been spared the loss of a few years of my life from the terror of having those horrors chasing me if only MacShaka had remembered that the *Et'moru* were from Gliesium's dark side and had pretty good night vision.

I was beside myself and promptly flounced off in a rage to find a quiet corner to weep in fear and frustration. I did not know what I had done to receive such careful attention from MacShaka. It seemed there was some primal urge within him to expose me to death at every opportunity. He could have picked anyone for his foray into the woods and the attendant attempt by the *Et'moru* to slaughter us for our troubles – anyone who wasn't already torn up with fractured ribs and who had not just survived an encounter with the *Chúsheng* but also a massacre by the *Athand'u,* and an intimate attempt at beheading by an *Et'moru* warrior. He did not, however; he simply picked me.

It was a curious condition of my service to him – his need to send me into the breech at every opportunity. In my short time, he had dragged me everywhere and thrust me into every danger. What stands out are the adventures that he personally arranged for me; his pairing me with the prospector, Fremantle Freya, and sending me in with a score of the *Ossayuln* tribe of Gliesiuns to take on a band of Black Hand bandits for one. That I had to endure a Blood Ritual that had me stripped naked and painted scarlet was just window dressing to the horrid event. Or my accompanying him to Gleann Fearadadh with the War Chief Amandeep MacGrogan-Singh to convince his gang of savages to join us in an attack on a Black Hand fort in the Coloe Vallis. That I was voluntold to join in a 'Dance', a type of *Bruicheath* or battle dance, with a massive Yeti-sized warrior named O'Sullivan that nearly cost me my life, was just part of the adventure. Yes, MacShaka truly had something in for me that belied his passing concern each time he pulled me back from the dead.

I had little time for excessive melancholy, however, for the *Et'moru* were moving in force and it was all hands to the barricades as we prepared for the attack. I joined Fung Wai-ting and Usman at the window above the gates. The shutters were wide open and both of them were crouched behind a thick stack of wood.

"*Dost,*" Usman said with the devil-may-care grin that I was so envious of, "come sit by us." Wai-ting had her back to the defences with her knees up to her chin and her rifle resting on the wood. She glanced at me, shy as she was, and said nothing. She did, however, which was much out of character, offer me a small smile. Usman shifted her, moving her bodily so that I could sit beside them. It was freezing in the darkness of night, at least -25 degrees. I was well dressed for it, with all of my uniform and *postin* to boot. I'd again opted for the heavy turban for more warmth, and I'd even had Jindan help me wrap it before Sittina whisked her away to a window on the west side of the building.

"You three watch the window!" Muneer snapped as he stalked by, his beard bristling and his eyes boring into us. He looked particularly dangerous beneath his black turban with the tail wrapped around his face for warmth. We made obedient, offered obsequious honourifics, then shifted around on our knees and faced the darkness beyond the window.

"Were they scary creatures?" Usman inquired as he scanned the darkness.

"They were fucking terrifying," I whispered.

"*Wǒ bù huì hàipà*," Wai-ting muttered in her tiny soprano voice.

"I know you won't," I replied. "You're fearless."

It was times like this, as I spared the 16 year old beside me a sympathetic glance, that I wondered at the morality of employing this bird-like girl to fight the United Nations' battles light years from Earth. She was a volunteer after a fashion; sold as she was by her relatives at the age of 12 to be a *wallah*, until she came of age. She could have bowed out when she turned 16 eight months before, but with no other opportunities before her save for slavery or prostitution – or both – she opted to stick it out. It meant, however, that the most unlikely of soldiers – myself, two 16 year old Chinese girls, Usman, and a number of others – were the fighters on the front line that night; hardly a reason for hope, when I put my mind to it.

"Well now, ain't ya'll got more guts than you can hang on a fence?" Bohman asked as he paused to stand before us. Usman and I faced him while shy Wai-ting remained looking out the window and acting like the responsible one. Bohman had a pair of heavy 9mm pistols on his belt, a 20 cm Bowie knife in a sheath, and a pulse rifle resting on one shoulder. Beneath his black Stetson and monumental moustache he winked and smiled – a cooler head you didn't see. "Gonna be a busy night tonight. Gotta slop the hogs, dig the well, and plow the south forty before breakfast."

Usman looked confused and I felt myself once again warming to the old buffer. "There'll be no grass growin' under our feet," I offered back and Bohman let out a long chuckle.

"God damn it, hoss, you could talk the hide off'n a cow. Hell, if you survive the night, you an' I are gonna get tighter 'n bark on a log."

I don't know why, but that made me feel so much better.

"Damn rights," I replied as I pulled out my pipe and stuffed it with *bhang*.

"You go easy on that stuff, hoss," Bohman added with a wink. "Too much an' you won't know 'come here' from 'sic 'em.'"

With that, he walked off to a point on the east side of the building.

I puffed on my pipe for a while, enjoying the calming effects of the *bhang*. Usman puffed occasionally, as did Wai-ting – she had the prettiest cough – and we waited in the cold. I was growing drowsy and relaxed when Jindan skipped up to me with that gap-tooth smile and plumped down beside me.

"*Ásha ásha, khar!*" Usman called out in an obnoxious whinny. Jindan's smile froze and I shook my head in pity.

"Oh, Usman."

The words had barely been uttered before she reached across me and belted poor Usman in the mouth.

"Akh!" Usman shouted as he gripped his lip. "You made me bleed, girl!" he groused dripping with both blood and indignity.

"I will make you bleed much more, *gandī bandara*," she uttered with her smile returning.

Usman got up to find a medikit while Wai-ting ignored the raucous proceedings and looked out the window.

"I cannot stay, Sikunder. Muneer will find me and make me go back to sit with Hong-miao."

"Don't let me stop you," I replied, playing it cool as I checked my rifle.

"You will be safe, my *bahadur*?" She fluttered her lashes and clasped her hands in front of her. It was rather sweet, though I was put off slightly by Usman's blood on her fist.

"You know I will try," I avowed, feeling decidedly self-conscious before those piercing eyes.

"That makes me happy," she replied. Jindan sat up taller, looked around at the jawans and constables who were oblivious to us, and then grasped my cheeks tenderly in her cold hands and kissed me long on the lips. "Of what use is the veil if you are going to dance," she said beaming.

"Uhh..."

"Hush, my *bahadur*," she breathed with a final kiss. "I will see you soon." With that she stood, flashed that ever present smile of hers, and dashed back to her side of the building.

"*Xiǎo dòng bù bǔ, dà dòng chī kǔ*," Wai-ting whispered as she continued to peer into the darkness.

I said nothing for a few moments as I fought between embarrassment, lust, and confusion. I had no idea what to do at this point, for I felt Jindan was more like an annoying little sister – or maybe a first cousin after that kiss. Having had little to do with the opposite sex, and even less success with that mysterious species, I was completely at a loss with one practically throwing herself upon me. What was I to do? I wondered.

"What did you say?" I finally asked.

"A small hole not mended in time," Wai-ting murmured as she wiped her nose, "will become a big hole much more difficult to mend." She looked at me with her dark almond eyes. "You should make up your mind, Sikunder."

"Yes," I agreed, "I must."

"*Armaan*," Usman said with a hint of pique as he returned with a scrap of bio-dressing on his lip. "Why did she do that?"

"I doubt it had anything to do with you calling her a donkey, Usman," I replied smiling and puffing on my pipe.

"*Ahk*, that was a joke, Sikunder. Your girlfriend cannot take a joke."

"She ain't my girlfriend, Usman," I shot back with less than convincing sincerity.

Usman nodded knowingly and resumed looking out the window.

"Oh dear," I said as I did the same. Why my life had to get so complicated right before its end I didn't know.

* * * * *

"They're coming from east!" a voice shouted.

I jerked awake, emerging from a *bhang* induced doze in an explosion of adrenalin that had my heart pounding fit to burst. The east, I thought frantically, which direction is that?

The far side of the compound.

Shots sounded in the darkness, muffled and distant. There were more shouts and suddenly a fusillade of shots from the jawans of Cong's contubernium.

"Mind yer fuckin' front!" MacShaka roared at me as he strode through the darkness barking orders and damning our eyes.

We didn't need further encouragement, for above the clatter of rifle fire and panicked shouts, we could hear the soul shattering shrieks in the darkness before us.

"Keep a close eye," I shouted as I waved the barrel of my pulse rifle back and forth. Within the forest, I could pick out the occasional flash in my thermal lenses as *Et'moru* gathered in the darkness. There was no point in shooting, however, for they were well over a 100 meters away and I was a poor shot at best and the *bhang* in my system only made it worse, if that were possible. A reasonable trade off, though, for at least I wasn't crying.

A snap sounded, and a splinter of wood the size of my thumb was blasted from the window frame. I ducked, hiding further behind the stacked wood. The wood itself was suddenly jostled, and several pieces fell upon us.

"Shit sakes," I shrieked as more shots fanned around us, ripping off strips of wood and punching into our log barricade. Wai-ting and I restacked the wood as quickly as possible while Usman fired a few shots into the night. The screams were growing louder and the incoming shots were increasing in volume.

"All three o' ye horn idle keelies fucking fire!" MacShaka roared as he knelt beside us and fired. I took a deep breath, stuck my head above the shattered windowsill, pointed my rifle, and fired at the first flash I saw. I doubt I hit it, but the racket the four of us were putting up seemed to cool the martial ardour of the *Et'moru* for a few moments, for their shots faded to nothing within a minute.

MacShaka looked closely at us. "Listen carefully now. They're attackin' the far side o' the convent, but it's a ruse. They'll be coming in force for the gate. The constables are hauldin' the gate, but you three need tae slow the bastards down. Get it?"

We nodded, and MacShaka offered me one of his bear strength shoulder claps that sent me sprawling before he charged away. I rubbed my arm and resumed my watch. We didn't wait long, for minutes later we suddenly saw dozens of white shapes near the tree line.

"Here they come!" I shouted as we fired. The *Et'moru* fired back for a moment, then suddenly dozens of their shrieking voices rose and a horde of the creatures emerged from the trees, sprinting across the snowy field with the speed of cheetahs. We fired only a few shots before they were at the gate. They were armed with *lanceis* and their throwing knives, and some carried pulse rifles. All carried *scutum* shields – which seemed to offer them some small degree of bullet resistance – and they were dressed in a hideous assortment of heavy wool *caparisons* and mismatched armour. The *Et'moru* were pounding on the gate below, throwing their bodies at it with a ferocity that defied imagination. They clawed, screamed, kicked, and butted against the wood slats, splintering them while the constables below shrieked and fired through the holes bored through the gate.

We fired down as best we could, but it was a regular donnybrook as the *Et'moru* fired at the windows and made an honest effort to climb the rough walls of the building in order to enter. Our shots were sporadic, for they were doing a fine job of keeping our heads down. Suddenly a screaming creature appeared over the sill, its *chamfron* mask a hideous carved face that I couldn't imagine being much uglier than the one beneath it. I howled in panic as I fired at it point blank; the creature screamed and disappeared below.

"*Shabash*!" Usman roared. "Well done, Sikunder!"

We continued to fire, but the *Et'moru* were clearly focusing all of their efforts on the gate. However, the score or so who charged the gate had been whittled down quickly enough, and as fast as they had charged, they retreated back into the woods leaving at least half of their number dead and dying. It was not much to show for a minute or two of fighting, but we'd held them off.

"Reload and be ready!" MacShaka barked. "Next time they'll come in numbers!"

I reloaded my rifle, shoved another magazine into my webbing, and crawled across the room to glance down into the courtyard below. The nuns were there, gathered in knots and whispering fearfully amongst themselves. All save for one. Coulthard stood alone, pulse rifle gripped tightly in her 60 plus year old hands as she looked upon the gates with a steely determination. She was immovable for a few more moments before she turned to her nuns and called out, "Hold your lines, sisters! Now is the time to fight!" The nuns did as they were told – eyes wide and terrified; two ranks, one kneeling, the second with rifles at the ready. Coulthard stood before them looking at each face. Suddenly she raised her pulse rifle over her head and called out in a loud clarion voice.

"O glorious Princess of the Heavenly Host, Saint Brigid, defend us in the battle and in the fearful warfare that we are waging against the Et'moru and their powers, against the rulers of this world of darkness, against the evil spirits!"

The nuns crossed themselves and bowed their heads.

"Come thou, to the assistance of these sisters, whom Almighty God created immortal, making them in His Own image and likeness and redeeming them at a great price from the tyranny of Satan!" She shook her rifle and her voice carried around the courtyard.

"Fight this day the battle of the Lord with thy legions of holy Angels, even as of old, thou didst fight against Lucifer, the leader of the proud spirits and all his rebel Angels, who were powerless to stand against thee!"

The nuns crossed themselves again, cheered with trembling voices, and then retook their fighting stances. Loosening limbs, checking their weapons, driving their feet into the snow for grip, the sisters knew that this time the *Et'moru* would break through and the fight would come to them. In minutes, the fate of the gleann and the thousands of humans and Gliesiuns now huddled and terrified at the doom that had come upon them would be decided by those 100 frightened nuns and their stubborn leader. The Cardinal of Gleann Ceallach, some wag had named her; it was hard to imagine a more fitting moniker.

"*Alexander Rutherford Armstrong*," lectured a dim voice in the back of my mind, "*how can you hold your head up high and allow a little old lady to fight for you?*"

Nana Armstrong had died seven months before I fled Earth. She'd had a stroke and lay in the baking sun beneath her apple trees for a couple of days before succumbing. It had been a horrible death, I thought, lying there alone with the knowledge that your end was coming – maybe not fast enough, but coming. I looked down upon Coulthard, tight lipped and focused, yet afraid; she was so very afraid. She was surrounded by her nuns, but at that moment I could see that she was very much alone.

"No one should die alone," I heard myself say as I stood and stalked over to the stairs and went down. I ignored the shouts of Usman as I rushed through the common room and out into the courtyard. I found myself standing before Coulthard who seemed oblivious until she caught sight of me from the corner of her eye.

"What are you doing here, Sikunder?" she asked as she returned her gaze toward the gate. The shrieks of the *Et'moru* resounded. They were coming.

"I'm here to fight," I returned as I took a place beside her. I pulled my pistol out, powered it up, heard the 'snick' as a round was chambered, then placed it back in its holster. I loosened my Khyber knife and hatchet, planted my feet, and tapped the button on the side of my rifle that released the 30 centimetre serrated bayonet.

"You should be with your own kind, Sikunder," she said through clenched teeth.

"I am," I replied.

"Nonsense," she muttered, though with much less asperity.

"Sacrifice," I replied. "You said to not question it. Generosity and sacrifice do not exist, you said, if no one benefits from it."

A small wintry smile crossed her lips. "Sikunder, you have bested me."

The constables suddenly opened fire through the holes in the gate and I brought my rifle to the ready.

"They come!" Coulthard cried. "*Glorious Saint Brigid, by thy protection, enable our souls to be so enriched by grace as to be worthy to be presented by thee to Jesus Christ, our Judge, at the hour of our death!*" she continued. A few of the nuns around us were weeping but Coulthard's voice drowned their fear away. "*As thou hast conquered Satan and expelled him from Heaven, conquer him again, and drive him far away from us at the hour of our death.*"

The gates shuddered beneath a mighty blow, and this time they bowed inwards while the constables pushed back.

"Be ready!" she roared.

The gates cracked, shimmied before the piled weight of the *Et'moru*, and then burst asunder. A roiling mass of *Et'moru* tumbled in, pouring like a living wave to wash through the breech and into the courtyard.

"Fire!" Coulthard shrieked as her nuns poured a volley into the turbid mass. Blood sprayed, limbs were shattered, pieces of armour were blasted apart, and the *Et'moru* shrieked in rage and agony.

"Fire!" Coulthard yelled again, and again the pulse rifles fired, shattering the *Et'moru* and blasting their numbers to hideous pieces.

"On your own, fire!"

Now the rifles kicked up a rare horror, punching into the mass, and shredding their bodies to crimson pulp. More *Et'moru* appeared behind them though and they fired over the shuddering bodies of their kin.

A nun screamed and fell clutching her stomach. A second dropped soundless, most of her face blasted off in a cloud of blood, brains, and bone; another fell shrieking while holding her arm now hanging by skin. The nuns' fire faltered and there were cries of dismay, fear, and rage; a few dropped their rifles to flee.

"Steady, sisters!" Coulthard screamed.

Suddenly *Et'moru* burst from the gory maw of the gate to spread left and right, descending upon our flanks with their *lanceis* swinging and their throwing knives zinging into the ranks of the nuns. We fell back into a smaller group, leaving the dying behind. The nuns fired, but it was hand to hand now; the *Et'moru* were amongst us. Here the nuns stood no chance, their pulse rifles useless at close quarters. The *Et'moru* ripped and slashed them to pieces.

My memories of those final moments are few, actually. I fired my rifle until it was empty and then stabbed and slashed until it was wrenched from my hands. A nun lay before me on her side, her face in a pool of blood as she hiccupped her life away and held the mess of her guts in her hands. An *Et'moru* writhed on its back as a nun pounded on its *chamfron* mask with the butt of her rifle while she screamed, "*O Mary, Queen of Heaven, procure for me the assistance of St. Michael at the hour of my death!*" With my Khyber knife in my left hand and my hatchet in my right, I faced down a bloodied *Et'moru* warrior with lance at the ready.

That particular memory is a curious one, more of a dream really, for at that moment when we locked in mortal hand-to-hand combat, reality was perverted and I watched from afar. The martial rage had me, a berserker explosion of hate as I parried its thrusts and blows and gave back as much if not more. I stabbed, slashed, swung, and kicked, beating the creature back until it lay on its side with my Khyber knife in its throat. (I gladly thank Klondikecorp for inundating my two months of hypersleep with every kind of cerebellum programming. Hand-to-hand combat was one of the few that seemed to have stuck – at least when I wasn't in a panic or being ambushed. I was not a bad hand at it in a stand up fight with a pipe load of drugs in my system.)

Soon enough I found myself on the ground with blood running down my face and a leg that wasn't working so well. The battle was at its height with the *Et'moru* locked and paired with the nuns. One creature lay dead before Coulthard, while another held her throat with its *lancea* poised. I threw myself at the creature, hatchet raised and a cry on my lips. The *Et'moru* thrust its lancea into Coulthard, dropped her, and swung upon me. Too late did it reach for its *scutum*, for my hatchet buried itself deeply into the side of its head. The creature fell, and I dropped to my knees beside Coulthard.

Her eyes were wide and unseeing; blood ran freely from her mouth.

She was dying.

From nowhere came a blow on the side of my head – a tail I suspect from the death agony of the *Et'moru* I had just tomahawked. It opened my already torn ear afresh and new blood ran down my face. I was suddenly on my hands and knees fighting for my consciousness. For a moment I looked upon the cold icy face of Coulthard; she still stared into the darkness above. I fell to my side, the inviting darkness of unconsciousness fast approaching. I gripped her hand in mine and squeezed.

Coulthard squeezed back.

"I'm here, Nana," I found myself whispering. "I'm here," I repeated.

A roaring sound was in my ears, and I lay my head in the cooling snow.

"You're not alone, Nana."

I closed my eyes to the horror of the battle and to the screams of the dying. When I opened them a moment later, I lay on my side upon a carpet of wonderfully fragrant and recently clipped verdant lawn. Above me, snowy white sheets fluttered in a kiln dry wind while leaves in a score of apple trees rustled like the sound of a long distant cheer. The sun beat down; mercilessly warm after the frigid skies of Samsāra. I looked to my left and there lay my grandmother, her hand in mine and her face serene, lacking the morose mannerisms I remembered so clearly.

"I'm here, Nana."

My grandmother rolled her head slowly and gazed upon me with eyes placid in approaching death. A small smile crossed her dried lips.

"Hello, Alexander," she whispered. "I've missed you."

"I missed you to, Nana." Tears welled in my eyes.

"You're a good boy, Sikunder, to come back for me," Nana said as her head rolled back to face the sky. She closed her eyes and said again, "You're a good boy."

Reverend Mother Mary Margaret Coulthard lay in the snow, a smile playing on her lips as she closed her hand tightly upon mine.

"Thank you, Sikunder," she murmured. She said nothing more.

The darkness was nearly complete and I closed my eyes to the beguiling comfort that death always offered as I faced it down. The last sounds I heard were more shots, the deep base roar of "*Victor Panthera Centuria*!", and then wonderful, intoxicating nothing.

* * * * *

My eyes opened.

The darkness faded and a blur of fantastic images began to appear; fire and movement, light and darkness.

I was lying on my chest in the snow.

"*Victor Panthera Centuria*!"

"Sikunder!" It sounded hollow, as if my name was being shouted down the length of a tunnel. I felt hands grasp me, roll me over, and then support my limp form.

"Sikunder!"

Usman was crying.

"Sikunder! *Dost*! My friend!"

Usman's tears should have terrified me but I was awash in such a splendid euphoria that they didn't bother me at all.

"Sikunder, please!" He was holding me tight, looking desperately for help. Fresh tears rolled down his cheeks and his shoulders shook. "Sikunder, my brother, please don't go."

Darkness slowly returned.

* * * * *

"Come on, Sikunder, hang on."

More dull words, and when I opened my eyes it was to see Sittina kneeling beside me, her motherly visage worried as she held her rifle close. Beyond her were the climactic thrashings of hand-to-hand combat between the *Et'moru* and the Legion. Screams, cries for help, and horrific howls.

A light snow was falling, illuminated by the torches and fires. The nuns lay dying, dozens of still forms.

Usman was still crying.

Fung Wai-ting brushed blood from her nose and fumbled with a bio-dressing. Her hands shook so that she couldn't tear it. She dropped it, brushed more blood from her nose, then stood and walked away.

I closed my eyes.

* * * * *

"Rally round, ye Scarlet Bastards! *Victor Panthera Centuria*!"

Usman held me close, whispering to me in Pashto through his tears. Sittina was shooting the devilish figures in the darkness, and Muneer stood over me with his pistol and dripping Khyber knife.

"A mouth that praises and a hand that kills, *Mashallah*!"

Torches flickered over the piled corpses. There weren't many of us left.

* * * * *

My eyes opened.

The torchlight was blotted by the shadow of MacShaka, Khyber knife in one hand and a hatchet in the other as he stood before me. He was facing the *Et'moru*. He drew a deep breath and bellowed:

> "*Fye now Johnnie, get up and run,*
> *The Highland bagpipes mak a din,*
> *It's better tae sleep in a hale skin.*
> *For 'twill be a bloody morning!*"

MacShaka roared a wordless cry as he charged the *Et'moru*. The creatures fell back in fear at the raging bear that bore into them. I felt a grin form. MacShaka would be glad to die in such a way. I glanced at Usman as my eyesight blurred and began to darken. His eyes were closed and he was praying. His tears were falling still, and he held me close in a brotherly love that warmed me. I glanced at Coulthard; I still held her hand. Her grey face was composed and her eyes were closed.

The Cardinal of Gleann Ceallach was gone.

My Nana was gone.

The darkness returned.

*****

"See you, lad," said a deep voice penetrating the darkness, "but this daes get tiring after awhile."

There were more words, muffled and incomprehensible, which was often what MacShaka sounded like, even when I was fully conscious. Finally, my eyes fluttered open and I found myself lying on my side on a sleeping mat in the common room.

"Ye were far through, I thought again," MacShaka said as he sat on the floor beside me. He was a much battered cave bear – his arm in a sling, his head and a hand bandaged. He was weary looking as well, as if the weight of the world lay upon him.

"Did we win?" I asked with a voice thick and groggy.

"Aye," he sighed. "We held 'em off. They're gone now and I doubt we'll see them again soon."

"Did we lose anyone?" I asked.

MacShaka looked at me and nodded. "Aye, lad, we daed."

*****

Jindan lay on a mat in a corner, a wool blanket pulled over her tiny body. I sat beside her long into the morning weeping as if my very heart had broken. I had lost many comrades since coming here, but the sting of this one was the most painful. The stirrings of love had been there I believe, deeply buried beneath my adolescent angst and insecurity; now it was too late.

She was gone.

Some time in the morning, MacShaka sat beside me as I wept and placed a fatherly arm around me. In that moment, as I leaned against him and buried my face in his beard while he comforted me, I knew that everything that hulking buffalo of a man asked of me, he repaid with everything I needed from him.

I was no longer alone.

* * * * *

The Cardinal of Gleann Ceallach was buried with 83 of her nuns in the days that followed. I look back fondly on that woman, so very much like my Nana Armstrong. Strong and determined, a true inspiration in her own way, yet sadly alone. I never found out much about her, but I was thankful for the opportunity to be with her at her end. I discovered that I had harboured a lot of guilt for missing the death of my Nana, knowing that it had been horrible and that she had been alone. Perhaps it was that guilt which had inspired me to stand with the Cardinal, to be, if nothing else in this life, the companion of someone who is alone and about to die.

We buried our own in the castrum, a new cemetery for a new fort. We lost nine jawans including my Jindan and Fung Wai-ting. The pain did not diminish in the coming days, and what guilt I had assuaged over the loss of my Nana, I replaced with my unrequited love for a young Hindu girl named Jindan Chandrakala.

Life is full of regrets I've found as I write these memoirs, and the worst are those that you create yourself through indifference and fear. I wish I'd learned that bitter lesson much earlier in my life.

The End

About the author:

Sean Pól MacÚisdin grew up in the Okanagan Valley, British Columbia, enjoying the outdoors and the simple life before choosing a career in the Canadian Navy. Although he saw many countries during his career, it is the fjords and bays of the coast of British Columbia that inspire him most with their rugged beauty and awesome sense of isolation. Although his writing career was slowed by his time at sea and raising a family, it has renewed itself in the world of the ebook.

Connect with Me Online:

Twitter: SeanMacUisdin
Facebook: Author Sean MacÚisdin
Smashwords: Sean MacÚisdin
My blog: seanmacuisdin.wordpress.com
Amazon Author Page: Sean MacÚisdin
Other books published by this author:

Europa Rising: The Divine Hammer
Jupiter Rising: The Columbus Protocols
The Scarlet Bastards – A Company Soldier

Made in the USA
Charleston, SC
14 September 2015